Spies in Disguise

Kate Scott was born in London. She has lived in Hong Kong, Paris, Scotland, and two tiny villages in France. She now lives in Dorset with her husband and two children.

Kate writes children's books, children's television programmes, radio plays and poetry. She's had lots of different jobs but now she makes up stories – the best job in the world.

She likes drawing, dancing, reading and 1940s films. She hates raw tomatoes and being tickled.

Sometimes her children read what she's writing and give her advice on how to make it better.

Spies in Disguise

BOY IN TIGHTS

Kate Scott

Piccadilly Press

Dedicated to the memory of Margaret Carey:
a dear friend, a warm wit,
a generous spirit,
an outstanding talent

First published in Great Britain in 2013
by Piccadilly Press,
A Templar/Bonnier publishing company
Deepdene Lodge, Deepdene Avenue,
Dorking, Surrey, RH5 4AT
www.piccadillypress.co.uk

A catalogue record for this book is available
from the British Library

ISBN: 978 1 84812 349 6

1 3 5 7 9 10 8 6 4 2

Printed and bound by CPI Group (UK) Ltd, Croydon, CR0 4YY
Cover design by Simon Davis
Cover illustration by Clare Elsom

Chapter 1

Dan McGuire – secret agent, supreme genius – would never put up with this. Dan McGuire is cooler than ice cubes. Dan McGuire decides his own bedtime. Dan McGuire would give my mum one look and she'd crumble like cake.

Unfortunately, Dan McGuire isn't here.

Dan McGuire only exists in books.

I've just walked through the door – I haven't

even put my school bag down – when Mum hits me with it. I came home looking forward to getting a stack of sandwiches and settling down in front of the telly. Instead, I've been ambushed by Mum and Dad in the hall.

'We're moving – *today*?' I repeat after her. 'You're joking.' I scan her face for telltale twitches – any signs that she's trying to be funny.

Not even a nostril flare. In fact, she's looking pretty scary.

'I'm not joking.'

No explanations, no apologies. No preparation, no packing, no estate agents. No discussions, no warning. No nothing.

'We can't move just like that!' I say.

'No time for drama,' Dad replies. 'We need to get a move on.'

I take a deep breath – I need to talk to them carefully, in case they're not just crazy, they're actually dangerous. 'We can't just *leave*.'

'We'll tell you everything when we get there, Joe,' Dad says. His voice is low and urgent, like he's in a disaster film at the point they tell you the volcano's about to blow.

That's when I see the two suitcases and small bag by the front door.

Maybe you shouldn't argue when the volcano's about to blow.

'What about my stuff?' If they've packed for me there's no way they haven't left something important behind.

'Joe . . .' Mum starts.

'Let him go, Zelia,' Dad says.

Mum taps her watch. 'Thirty seconds.'

I run. I have the washing-machine-stomach feeling I get before anything big happens. The problem is, I don't know if this is the start of an adventure – like when Ryan Jackson's parents decided to move the family to Australia – or the beginning of a nightmare – like when Connor Forsey had to have two teeth taken out after putting toothpaste on his tongue instead of using a toothbrush for a year.

Upstairs, I look round my room – at all my

football posters, at my ancient washed-out duvet with the miniature planes on it that I've never let Mum throw out, at the pile of Dan McGuire Secret Agent books I know off by heart. Wherever we're going, it can't be for long if they've left all my stuff. The thought calms me down. Sort of.

I grab my football from the cupboard and my kit bag from the floor (how could they *not* have packed my football?) and stuff in as many Dan McGuire books as I can. I go back down the stairs three at a time.

In the hall, Mum grabs my arm as I turn towards the front door. 'Not that way, Joe.'

A mobile phone rings once and then cuts off.

'That's our signal,' Dad says. 'We've got to get out of here – now!'

'Here.' Mum shoves a balaclava at me as Dad picks up the suitcases. 'Put this on.'

'You want me to look like a thief?'

'Just do as your mum says,' Dad snaps. Dad hardly ever gets annoyed – what's going on?!

I tug on the too-small balaclava until my head's trapped in the woollen vice. My eyes are bugging out of the tiny eyeholes. This could be one of those TV programmes where they convince some idiot that something brilliant is happening. Then the idiot has to pretend to laugh when it turns out it's all a practical joke.

I hope I'm not the idiot.

'Come on,' Mum says, thrusting the small bag at me to take.

We leave the house the back way. There's a long, shiny black car parked in the lane. The car bleeps and Mum and Dad slide in, gesturing for me to get in the back. It's sleek, new, clean. Nothing like the car we used to have – the one Dad nicknamed Snack for Scrap.

'On the move,' Dad murmurs. He's talking into the smallest phone I've ever seen. It's silver, about the size of a credit card and almost as thin.

Mum starts the car and eases out into the street.

Seconds later we're swinging onto the main road.

I lean forward, putting my face between the two front seats. Dad points his phone at the dashboard and clicks. Panels slide back to reveal dozens of tiny red and green flashing lights, buttons and switches. A large blue screen in the dashboard shows a squiggle of roads, and a little red dot blinks along one of them. I guess that little red dot is us.

I touch the seats – they're soft and smooth instead of rough and sticky and covered in crumbs. Why couldn't Mum and Dad have picked me up from school in *this*?

'Sit back, sweetheart.' Mum glances into the rear-view mirror. 'And tighten your seatbelt.'

Before I can reply, Mum makes a sudden gear change and I'm thrown against the back of my seat. The car's wheels screech as she takes a hard right, then a left, then another right. I grab hold of the door handle as I'm swung from side to side. This is *Mum* driving? The woman who thinks you shouldn't drive faster than someone with a Zimmer frame can walk?

Mum swerves around another corner.

'Are we in a car chase?' I manage to ask, after my face meets the back seat for the third time.

'We'll talk about it later, Joe. You all right back there?' Dad sounds cheery now, almost but not quite like the dad I remember from before today. 'You can take the balaclava off now. Relax.'

Relax? But I pull off the balaclava. We're on the motorway now and Mum's really putting her foot down. She zips through to the fast lane and stays there. If we were in a Formula One race Mum would *definitely* be winning.

This is totally blinding!

Dad jabs at the buttons on the dashboard. It's obvious he knows the car's controls back to front. The dad who used to fumble with the petrol cap and stall the car on hills has gone.

As we whip along the motorway, speeding past the kind of cars I used to watch speeding past us, I can't help wishing my best friend Eddie could see me. Up until today, Mum and Dad have been cup-of-tea-and-a-biscuit-in-front-of-the-telly, ordinary parents. I watch the red dot pulse across the screen as Mum weaves through the lanes and Dad jabs at buttons like a professional computer hacker. There's no way I can call them ordinary now.

All of a sudden, Mum and Dad are strangers.

Chapter 2

I've just launched into a new round of questions when a piercing bleep sounds and *CODE ES3503* scrolls across the top of the screen. A green dot appears behind our red dot.

Dad flicks a bunch of switches with the tips of his fingers and a video image of a car flashes up on screen. 'It's a Corsa. Red. Index NE16 S06. It's getting close.'

'Not for long, it isn't,' Mum says. She guns the engine and swings back over to the fast lane. My seatbelt cuts into my chest as we surge forward. Mum zips from lane to lane. We're going so fast the streetlamps blur but the gap between the red and the green dot widens as Mum speeds ahead. On a 'this is brilliant' scale of one to ten, this is *eleven*.

Dad's phone bleeps and he reads a message. 'Back-up's installing some roadworks. If you can keep up the speed for another four minutes we'll be out of danger.'

Mum laughs. 'No problem.'

Dad used to call Mum the Couch Potato Princess. Now she's acting like a speed demon. *Where's my mum gone?!*

I'm pushed even further back into my seat as Mum puts her foot to the floor. We whip by signs so fast I can't even read them.

The green dot slows to a stop and then

disappears from the edge of the screen. 'We're in the clear,' Dad tells us.

'Excellent,' Mum says. 'I won't even have to double back.' She slows down – slightly – and takes the next exit. A few minutes later we draw to a stop.

I peer out of the tinted window. We're parked in front of a squat, dirty brown building. It looks like an enormous toad. A small yellow neon sign is flashing *Stacey's Self-service Motel*.

'I'll check us in.' Mum cuts the engine.

I notice a black iron fire escape zigzagging up the side of the building. In *Dan McGuire Meets the Agent of Doom*, Dan is chased down fifty floors of a fire escape, taking the last flight in one leap. At this point, I wouldn't be surprised if Mum and Dad do something similar.

Mum slips out of the car, closing the door gently behind her. She glances from left to right and then walks up to a steel panel next to the motel's front door and presses some buttons.

'What's happening?'

Dad ignores me. He's taken his miniature phone out of his pocket. 'First destination,' he says into it.

As Dad tucks the phone out of sight, Mum beckons us from the door, which is now open. Dad's out of the car before I've even undone my seatbelt. I didn't know he had it in him to move that fast.

'Come on.' Dad's holding the small bag and is glancing around the car park as if he's watching out for something. I keep close to him – I have a feeling I don't want to find out what that something is.

Mum and Dad bundle me through the door and more or less push me along the corridor. It smells of mould and cat wee and is painted a green that reminds me of school. Not in a good way. All the room doors are a matt grey, with a keypad next to them. The person who designed this place probably does prisons and schools as well.

We stop at a door at the end of the corridor,

next to a fire exit. Mum jabs at the keypad, and the door gives a soft click. She sticks her head in, looks round, then yanks at my arm to pull me inside.

'Hey!'

'Shhh,' Dad hisses from behind me.

Once we're inside, the door closes softly behind us. To the left there's a double bed with a dirty orange cover, and another single bed by the window in front of us. The curtains are made from the same grubby orange material covering the beds. The smell of mould and cat wee is really strong now.

Whatever's happened to Mum and Dad must be bad if this is the kind of place we'll be staying in. I go over to the single bed and sit down. The mattress sags down so far it almost touches the ground. I'm not sure I'll be able to get up.

Then Mum and Dad start acting weird again – or weirder.

Dad goes over to the window and draws the curtains. Then he picks up and peers at the lamps, examines the earpiece of the room's phone, checks under the beds. Mum takes the drawers out of the side table and examines the inside. She turns the drawers over before sliding them back in.

Eventually they seem to get tired of ransacking the room.

'Right.' Dad sits down on the double bed. 'Time to talk.'

Mum sits down next to him and clasps her hands around her knees.

I sit up as straight as I can on the sagging bed. 'Are we running away from the police?'

'No!' Mum's got a bit of a nerve looking shocked at my suggestion.

'We haven't done anything wrong,' Dad says.

'You said we're in trouble,' I point out.

'We are, but it's because of other people.' Dad draws out his words as if testing them to see how much they give away. 'The thing is, I'm not a political consultant. And your mother isn't a computer programmer.'

'We're spies,' Mum says.

'What?!' I don't know what I was expecting but it definitely wasn't *this*.

Dad glares at Mum.

She shrugs. 'We had to tell him.'

'I was planning on leading up to it a bit,' he says.

'HANG ON!'

Mum and Dad jump.

'*Spies?*' Dad doesn't look anything like James Bond – any of them – and Mum . . .

I stop and consider their black clothes, the small black case and the drawn curtains.
I think of the fast, smart car outside.

Yeah, they look exactly like spies.

'We've been working undercover for so long we didn't think we'd have to move again,' Mum says. 'We moved all the time before you were born.'

I open my mouth. Then I shut it again.

'I know it's a bit of a shock, but we're on the run,' Mum says, reaching down to tug at her boots. She pulls one off and fiddles with the heel. It pops open and she empties out a small metal object. She tosses it to Dad. He catches it neatly with one hand.

'Sensor,' Dad says, as if that's an explanation.

Dad gets up and sticks the object in the centre of the door, where it winks at us with a small green light.

'You're not kidding, are you?'

'No. We're not,' Dad says.

'You're really spies?'

'We're really spies,' Mum says.

'And we're not going home.'

'I'm sorry, Joe,' Dad says. 'But our covers have been blown. We're going to have to go somewhere else and become new people for a while.'

'How long for? You mean, *for ever*?'

Dad crouches down in front of me and puts his hand on my shoulder. 'We might move on again but we can never go back to where we were, no.'

'It's just too dangerous,' Mum says, her voice

soft. 'Believe me, we wouldn't be doing this unless we had to.'

I gaze at the swirly green and orange carpet. On the one hand, I'm never going back to my old life again. There's my friend Eddie – I'll miss Eddie. And I really wish I'd packed up *all* of my Dan McGuire book collection.

But on the other hand, I can expect car chases and spy gadgets and cool black outfits. I can expect the kind of stuff that happens to Dan McGuire on a daily basis. Fizzy drinks by swimming pools, travelling on high-speed trains and planes in first class, having the FBI shake your hand and say, 'Good work, son.' Maybe there's even a five-a-side team for all the kids of the spies. Or maybe we'll have to move to Brazil on diplomatic spy business and I'll get talent-spotted by my favourite football team of all time – Santos. Maybe the team will all sign my shirt.

So long, Eddie.

'This is going to be *great!*'

Dad coughs. 'Yeah. The thing is . . .' He trails off, glancing at Mum.

Mum pushes her hair behind her ear. 'The thing is, our new cover story means a few changes.'

'Quite big changes.' Dad doesn't seem to want to catch my eye.

'A new house. A new school.' Do they think I don't get it?

'Yes,' Mum says. But she looks awkward too.

Before I can ask why, a low, metallic voice speaks. 'Subject four metres away.'

 Mum and Dad swivel towards the door. The sensor is flashing blips of red light. 'Subject three metres away.' I realise the voice is coming from the sensor.

Dad pulls the curtains and opens the window. Mum swishes the bag along the floor towards Dad. Dad picks it up and fishes out a coil of metal rope with a hook at the end of it. He attaches the hook to the windowsill and drops the cable out of the window. Then he gestures me towards it.

'Out there?' I whisper.

Dad nods. 'Wait until I tell you to go,' he whispers back. He holds his finger up to his lips.

The metallic voice speaks again, this time more softly. 'Subject less than one metre away.'

That's pretty cool, a gadget that knows when to lower its voice.

Mum ducks into the bathroom and sets the taps running in the bath.

There's a sharp knock on the door.

Mum detaches the sensor from the door and slips it into her pocket.

Another knock.

I really hope Mum and Dad are good at their job.

Mum waves to Dad, who bends down and picks up the boot she'd taken off and flings it across the room. She catches it neatly and pulls it back on as there's a third rap on the door.

'Yes?' Mum shouts over the noise of the running water.

From the other side of the door there's a deep voice. 'Room service.'

'I think there's been a mistake. I didn't order any room service.'

'No mistake. It's on the house,' the deep voice says.

Dad pulls me close, whispering in my ear. 'I'll give you a leg up. Go and get in the red car next to the space we were in.'

'But that's not —'

'Have to keep them guessing,' Dad tells me.

'Sure.' I do my best to act as if I'm always being asked to jump out of windows and into strange cars.

'Fast as you can. Here are the keys.' He pushes them into my hand. 'Press the button on the keyring when you get near it.'

'Where are you going?' Blood's rushing in my ears.

'We'll be right behind you,' Dad says. 'Now go.'

He hoists me up and almost in the same movement, I'm sliding down the wire to the tarmac below. I land and pelt towards the red car, holding out the keyring and jabbing the button. The car bleeps and the driver's side door swings open. As I dive in, the engine starts up by itself. I look back and see Mum and Dad crossing the car park, running fast. I scramble into the back seat and click my seatbelt. I've got the hang of this enough to know I'll need to be strapped in tight. Within a second of them getting in, we're screeching out of the car park. Mum speeds down a series of narrow winding lanes. There aren't any street lamps and we're skidding round sharp bends in the pitch black, but Mum doesn't let that slow her down.

'Well, that was an amateur outfit,' Mum says. 'Didn't even have anyone watching the window.'

'Not completely amateur.' Dad taps the screen where a new green dot is blinking behind our red one.

Mum sighs. 'Oh well. I guess that's to be expected.' She sounds like she's talking about a bad weather forecast, not about being chased by enemy spies!

She revs the engine and we screech around another corner. 'Hang on.'

I always thought a high-speed escape would be exciting but actually it's making me feel a bit ill. My face is squashed flat against the window as Mum takes a spectacularly sharp corner. I manage to speak out of the side of my mouth. 'Are they coming after us?'

'They can try.' Mum sounds cheerful, as if she likes the idea of a proper chase. My old mum didn't even like putting her foot down on bumper cars. It's going to take a while to get used to this new version.

'We weren't going to stay at the motel for long anyway,' Dad calls back to me. 'It's what we call a destination decoy.'

'We weren't going to stay there?' It's been a long day. I'm finding it hard to keep up.

'Of course not!' Mum says. 'I wouldn't be caught dead sleeping on those manky sheets!' Mum spins the wheel to turn another corner.

'They won't catch us, will they?' I don't fancy meeting Mum and Dad's enemies without having some training first. And a couple of their gadgets.

'Don't worry. Your mum's an old hand at this. Usually we wouldn't have expected them to find us so quickly, but they were slightly more ahead of the game than we expected.'

'Not *that* ahead of the game,' Mum says. 'Honestly – room service? As if!'

'You don't get room service in a self-service motel, do you?'

'Exactly.'

The gap between the two dots widens. Once the dot disappears from the screen, Mum heads back to the motorway (which at least means no more swerving round bends). Then she sweeps into the fast lane and overtakes any car that has the cheek to get in front of her.

'Back-up have tracked them down,' Dad murmurs to Mum.

I lean back and watch the cars swooshing past. Normal cars with their normal people on their way to normal places.

Not like my family. We're spies on the run – in serious danger.

How FANTASTIC is that?

Chapter 3

Mum and Dad are sitting opposite me on the edge of their bed. They keep shifting their positions and glancing at each other.

We arrived at the second motel in the middle of the night – the room had sheets that Mum approved of. Even the sensor liked it – it stayed silent for the rest of the night, or what was left of it. Now it's morning but I could do with at least another four hours of sleep. I push up my eyelids with my fingers and yawn loudly. Maybe they'll get the hint and let me go back to bed.

'You have to understand, we need to change our identities,' Dad starts. 'If we're going to stay safe it's vital that no one can recognise us.'

'They could be watching us, following us, at any time.' Mum glances at the sensor and I shiver, even though the room is hot and stuffy.

I really get it now – my old life is gone: Eddie; the football team; my teacher, Mr Burnside; Saturday mornings in the park; nice, ordinary parents. It's all gone for good.

Mum takes a breath. 'You remember Cousin Andrea?'

'Yeah, course I remember her,' I say, wondering what Cousin Andrea's got to do with anything. Cousin Andrea sometimes comes over to see Mum and Dad. She's always in a state about something and it's always 'private'. Mum and Dad have to have long whispered conversations with her in the kitchen. The only good thing about it is that they send me to the fish and chip shop to keep me out of the way. I guess that's gone now too.

'Cousin Andrea,' Mum says, 'isn't exactly what she seems.' She tugs at her ear. 'Cousin Andrea is actually Special Agent Andrew.'

'What?!'

'She's a man, Joe,' Dad says. 'She – I mean, he – is an undercover agent.'

I think back to all the times I've seen Cousin Andrea. I picture those big hands, the shapeless dresses, the thick, hairy legs. My mind races.

There's a reason they're telling me this.

And I see the expression in their eyes and I understand what that reason is.

No. They won't really say it. They can't! They wouldn't dare.

'It's often a part of going undercover,' Dad says.

'You're starting your new school as a girl,' Mum says quickly.

If my eyes were laser beams I'd be burning holes in Mum's face. 'No. Way.'

'Yes,' says Mum.

'Absolutely NO WAY!'

'It won't be hard to remember your new name because it's so like your old one – Josephine,' Mum goes on. 'So that's one good thing.'

Josephine?! A *good* thing?!

'We can call you Josie for short. That's pretty.'

'You can stop right there.' I give Mum the laser glare again. 'I'm not doing it.'

Mum lasers me back. 'Yes, you are.'

'Honestly, we feel really bad about this.' Dad looks like he means it, but what good is that?

'Why can't I change my hair? Have a different name? You can call me anything you like. I'll take Reginald! Brian! Nigel! I don't care, just don't make me be a girl!'

Mum's eyebrows dart up in warning.

I lower my voice. 'Please.'

'Think about it. It makes sense. Most people wouldn't believe it's possible to disguise a boy as a girl,' Mum says. 'They'd think that no boy would agree to it.'

'THAT'S BECAUSE THEY'RE RIGHT!'

27

'So when they're searching for a family of three with a son, your disguise as a girl will be what keeps us safe,' she finishes up.

'We have to throw them off our trail, Joe,' Dad says, spreading out his hands.

'Then why can't I stay behind? I could stay with someone. Anyone!'

Mum and Dad become very still.

'Don't you want to be with us?' Mum says, and for the first time she sounds not business-like, not like a spy, or a stranger, but like my mum. My mum when she's upset.

'Yes, of course I do,' I say quickly. Just not as a girl.

'We wouldn't be asking you to do this if we weren't in danger,' Dad says.

'A lot of danger,' Mum adds.

For Dan McGuire, danger means escaping on a jet, or in a high-speed train, or in a Lexus LFA. Apparently, for me it means prancing about in a dress.

But if we're in real trouble . . . I have to at least consider helping. I'd be saving Mum and Dad from the enemy.

'How long would I have to do this for?'

'Well,' Dad says, 'until we're sure we haven't been tracked to our new location. Three to six months, say.'

'Three to six months! Three to six *months*!' They have got to be kidding!

'Calm down,' Mum says. 'It probably won't be that long anyway. It's just until things go back to normal. And until back-up track down the people after us.'

'We wouldn't ask if it wasn't serious.' Dad pulls at his beard. 'We're only doing this for your own protection.'

'My own protection!'

'Stop repeating everything we say,' Mum says. 'Honestly, can't you think of it as a bit of fun?'

There's no way Dan McGuire would go down without a fight. It's time to make myself understood. Danger or not, there are some lines you don't cross.

'I am never, ever, *ever* going to wear a dress.'

Fifteen minutes later, I'm standing in front of the mirror in the tiny bathroom. My scalp itches. Bright yellow hair hangs down around my face like shiny spaghetti. I reach up to scratch.

'Don't do that! You'll make the wig wonky and give the game away.'

'But it's really itchy!'

'Well, do it *carefully* then,' Mum says. 'I'm sorry we can't curl and dye your hair but it's too short. It has to be a wig.'

'This. Is. My. Worst. Nightmare.'

Mum just smiles and smooths down my wig.

Some of the boys at my school have friends who are girls. I'm not one of them. How can I pretend to be something I don't even understand?

The Santos team back in Brazil are never going to sign my shirt now.

'Now the dress,' Mum says. 'Arms up.'

I stick my arms up in the air as if I'm being

arrested. Except being arrested would be better –
at least I'd be allowed to wear trousers.

To make things even worse, it's a pink dress – a
pink dress with *frilly* bits. It's the kind of dress my
sister would wear. If I had a sister. Mum slips it
over my head.

'It's like wearing a tent! My legs are freezing!'

'Then put on the tights.' Mum hands them to
me. 'They'll cover them up.' She sighs. 'Pity you
developed hairy legs so early. Apart from that and
your feet, you've got a lovely feminine build.'

'Do you mind?! Hairy legs are normal, if you're a
boy!' It's true; I got hair on my legs before any
other boy in my school. And yes, I have bigger feet
than anyone else in my class. But that was never a
problem – until now.

The tights are like two snakes hanging down
from a gaping mouth – and they're about to eat my
legs alive. I hold them at arm's length. 'How am I
supposed to put these on?'

'Don't be a ninny,' Mum says. 'One leg at a time.'

I lift up one leg and make a stab at putting my

foot in the large hole. I get it in the large bit but then lose my balance as I push my toes further down one of the legs. I fall over with the snakes tangled round my ankles. 'This is so *stupid*.'

'Oh for heaven's sakes.' She pulls me up to standing and shows me how to roll each leg up so I can stick my toes in the foot of the tights. Eventually, I manage it.

The tights itch my thighs and it's still drafty under the dress. How do girls cope with it? Anything could crawl under there. And where are the pockets?

'You'll get used to it,' Mum says. She swivels me round. Looking in the mirror is like turning to see an awful accident. You don't want to but you can't help yourself.

I'm the ugliest girl I've ever seen.

'I. Look. Ridiculous.'

Dad appears at the door. 'How are we getting on? Oh. I see.' Dad's got a trying-not-to-laugh look on his face. 'Honestly, Joe, it's not that bad.'

'No. It's worse.'

'Well, I think you're very . . . pretty.' Mum adjusts my wig.

'Pretty!'

There's a strangled sound from Dad.

'Get yourself under control,' Mum tells him.

I grit my teeth. 'You know, lots of girls wear trousers.'

'I did tell your dad that,' Mum says, 'but I'm afraid he did all the clothes ordering while I was out.'

'There's no way we can risk trousers yet,' Dad says. 'Not until you're really convincing as a girl. People believe what they're presented with. We have to present them with nothing but girl.'

'Well, anyway, Josie,' Mum says, 'your dad and I will get our new disguises together and then we can go.'

'You don't need to call me that now.'

'We may as well get used to it as soon as possible.' She's wearing what I already think of as her Serious Spy look. 'It'll only take one slip-up for the secret to be out, and that's all the enemy needs to find us.'

Even Dad's stopped smiling. 'It's really not a joke.'

He's telling me!

Mum rummages in her bag and pulls something out. 'This might make you feel better. We know you've been wanting a mobile phone for ages —'

'I wanted it to call my *friends*. The ones we're *leaving*.'

Mum ignores me. 'So we got you a reward for being so understanding,' she says, placing a slim phone in my hand.

'Who says I'm being understanding? I'm only doing this so we don't get caught.' But since I've wanted a mobile since roughly for ever, I give her a smile, then I look down to check it out.

It's bright pink.

Chapter 4

In every Dan McGuire book, there's a True Stories section about real-life spies. While I'm waiting for Mum and Dad, I remember that in *Dan McGuire and the Code-Cracker*, the true story is about Lea de Beaumont, the alias of Chavalier d'Éon – a man who dressed up as a woman so he could spy on the Empress of Russia.

This does not make me feel any better.

Half an hour later, with help from some extra high heels and a bottle of hair dye, Mum's a tall redhead in a smart dress and jacket. Dad's beard is gone and he's wearing a suit. It's like they've been abducted by aliens and replaced with brand new versions of their old selves. I notice *their* new covers don't involve them being embarrassed to death. Only yesterday I was looking forward to showing off one day about having cool spy parents. Now I wish everything was how it used to be.

Dad plucks the still-quiet sensor from the door and chucks it to Mum. 'Well, we better get on the road, girls, we've got a way to go.'

He's talking about us. Girls. Mum and I are the 'girls'. For a second I can't breathe.

Out in the corridor, I have to learn to walk all over again. The tights make my legs feel prickly so I straddle, but then Mum tells me to stop walking like a cowboy. The dress makes *swish-swish* sounds against my legs, and because there are no pockets to plunge my hands into, my arms hang down by my sides like an orang-utan. My new long hair tickles my cheeks. It's a nightmare come to life.

When Dan McGuire went undercover in *Dan McGuire – Stunt Spy* he got to pretend to be a stunt man for a film star and do things like leap across seventy bikes using a motor-powered scooter. But there's no way Josie is going to be leaping across anything. Not in these tights.

Outside, Mum leads us through the car park to a dark green car.

'*Another one?*'

As we're driving away from the motel Mum explains. 'We have to switch everything: identities, cars, back story —'

'Back story?'

'The story of where we come from, who we are. You need to learn your new identity. What Josie is like.'

I sink down into the seat. I wonder what Eddie's doing now and whether I'll ever be allowed to contact him again. Right now he's probably playing football in the park. *He* doesn't have to learn how to be a girl. I can't believe I wanted him to see me in my new life – the thought of Eddie seeing me in this dress reminds me of how I felt after two goes on the Fear Factor fairground ride last summer.

Dad pops his head over the seat. 'I'll show you the controls for the car before we get to work. For a start, let's get your seat sorted out.' He leans forward and rests his hand on the dashboard for a moment. The dashboard glows under his fingers, enclosing them with neon green. As I watch, panels slide away to reveal six screens across the dashboard and hundreds of buttons.

'Whoa! This car's even better than the last one!'

'I know,' Dad says, grinning. 'Now, put your hand palm down next to you.'

Dad flicks a few switches and presses a button marked *Reader*. A moment later my seat's sliding forward. Dad's seat moves to the left. Now I'm almost level with Mum and Dad in the front.

Dan McGuire has a car seat like this in *Dan McGuire at Top Speed*. It pops up cans of fizzy drinks and chocolate bars through the armrests.

Maybe Mum and Dad can organise some customisation later.

I search around for any buttons that might make something brilliant happen – or get me out of here. 'Is there an ejector seat?'

'Only in the movies, Joe.' Dad fiddles with the dashboard panels. 'Okay. Let's have a look at our new home.'

On the middle screen a picture pops up of a detached house with a slate roof. There are flowers growing up around the front door like on those postcards you see on holiday.

It's not exactly the city flat with mirror-black windows I've been imagining. I was thinking more of something on the twenty-sixth floor with a lift that goes at seventy miles per hour and walls that slide back to show three-hundred-inch televisions like in *Dan McGuire and the Techno Tyrant*.

'You see? It isn't all bad, Josie.'

I groan and lean back. The gadgets are cool. The house looks okay. But I'll never get used to being a girl.

Dad brings up a screen of text. 'Josephine Lily Marcus. Born the sixteenth of November.'

'Lily?'

Dad ignores me. 'No brothers or sisters, uncles or aunts. All grandparents deceased.'

'What about Cousin Andrea?'

'Cousin Andrea's on a new mission,' Mum says. 'There is no Cousin Andrea.'

'Josephine has an allergy to chlorine which means she is never able to swim,' Dad continues. 'This has also added to a pre-existing fear of drowning which prevents her from approaching any open water whatsoever.'

'But I love swimming!'

'You can hardly go swimming now,' Dad says. 'Would give the game away a bit, wouldn't it?'

I picture myself in a bikini. It's enough to put me off swimming for life.

I scowl at my reflection in the window. 'Why don't you just put me down as loving make-up and be done with it.'

'Do you mind?' Mum says. 'What exactly do you think being a girl means?'

'It means I can't do anything I like. It means wearing stupid dresses and talking about make-up and . . . and . . . *pink stuff* all day long.' I punch down the material of my dress which is puffing up in the breeze from the air conditioning.

'I see we'll have to work on your attitude as well as your disguise,' Mum says sharply.

Dad coughs and runs through the details of my place of birth, the story of my family and the origin of my fear of water (a traumatic seaside incident when I was three years old). I scratch at the edge of my wig as I try to concentrate. It looks like I'm going to have an itchy head for the next three to six months.

Three to six months!

'Josie?'

I drag a 'yes' from my throat.

'Pay attention,' Dad says.

Four hours later, I know my new life story back to front, and we're drawing up in front of the postcard house.

As Mum parks the car, a girl with spiky blond hair slams her way out of a house across the road from our new cottage. She's wearing tattered jeans, trainers and a light blue sweatshirt. The kind of clothes I used to wear all the time. The kind of clothes I'd kill for now. When she sees our car she stops and sits on the wall, staring over at us.

'Seems we have a neighbour,' Dad says.

Mum turns to me. 'Don't talk to her,' she says. 'You're not ready yet.'

'Ready for what? Knowing how to ask her what her favourite shade of pink is?'

'Josie . . .' There's a warning note in Mum's voice.

'Okay, okay, I won't say anything.'

As we get out of the car, Mum smiles and waves at the girl. 'Hello!'

The girl half raises her hand in response. Then she gets down and walks up the hill at a very fast pace. Probably off to tell all her mates about the new funny-looking girl who's moved into town.

The really ugly, funny-looking girl.

Mum scoops a key from her pocket and opens the front door, gesturing for us to follow. 'Oh, Jed!' Mum exclaims. She's staring at the wood burner in the corner of the room. There's a wicker basket next to it piled high with chopped logs and kindling. The windows have deep sills and long curtains. There's a sofa against one of the walls. I slump down on it and stare at the wooden floor.

Mum comes over and rubs my shoulder. 'It's really not that bad.'

Yes. It really is.

Mum walks through to the kitchen. A second later I hear a high-pitched bleeping noise. Not the kind of bleep a microwave makes when it's heated your macaroni cheese – a spy gadget bleep. It's been less than twenty-four hours since Mum and Dad let me in on their secret and already I can tell the difference. So I've got the choice of staying on the sofa to prove to my parents that they've ruined my life, or following Mum to find out what kind of spy gadgets are in the kitchen. I get up and follow Mum. I may as well make the most of the situation.

Mum is standing in front of a large pine cupboard. The open door shows there are no shelves inside, just a black panel at the back. She presses some buttons on a silver keypad to the right of it and the panel slides open.

Mum jumps when she sees me. 'You can't come in here.'

'Why can't I —?'

'*Upstairs*,' Dad says. 'It's not a game. This is serious.'

I leave. When a Narnia cupboard appears in the kitchen, you have to agree – it's serious.

Upstairs there are two bedrooms and a small bathroom. I go into the room with the single bed. The walls are strawberry milkshake pink. The bedside table is pink. The duvet is pink with little red cherries. The lampshade is pink. It must be a rule – girls have to be surrounded by pink things *at all times.* I walk over to the window. The garden outside is perfect for a kick-about – wide, flat and bordered by tall hedges and trees. But who am I supposed to play with? If I were at home, I'd probably be in the park with Eddie, playing football and listening to him complain about his sister, Tilly. According to Eddie, girls are evil and only ever want to boss you about. And now I am one.

I sink down on the bed – also pink – and scratch my legs. The tights are making them itch almost as much as my head under the wig. So far being a girl seems to mean a lot of itching.

Mum and Dad appear. 'Don't scratch so —' Mum says as there's a ripping sound and a hole appears in the right leg of my tights. She sighs. 'Your first ladder,' she says. 'Be more careful next time.'

Yeah, because looking good is a real concern of mine.

'It'll all be better once you start school on Monday,' Mum says, looping an arm around my shoulders.

'What?' That's the day after tomorrow! 'I need time to adjust! This is a life-changing situation! I'm traumatised!'

Mum tilts her head to consider me. 'You might be a little bit in shock, yes.'

I let out a sigh of relief.

'But you're still going to school on Monday.'

Chapter 5

In *Dan McGuire and the Coiling Cobra*, Dan McGuire is trained to wrestle snakes and crocodiles in the middle of the River Nile, bare-handed. I should be so lucky.

Dad starts my girl training on Sunday by making me walk across the room with books on my head.

'I thought they only do this *in* books.'

'What's good enough for fiction is good enough for you.'

So much for Dad feeling bad about making me be a girl.

Luckily, Mum arrives and saves me as Dad's debating whether or not I should learn how to curtsey. 'What are you *doing*?'

'He's got to learn how to act the part, Zelia.'

'He's not going to a finishing school, Jed! It's a perfectly ordinary primary school.'

'Yes, but to convince everyone, he's got to be as feminine as possible. A really girly girl.' Dad reaches over and pinches my cheek. 'He's got to be our little princess.'

I just – I just can't speak.

'First of all, our son is not an actress or a dancer – it's a big enough challenge for him to learn how to put on a pair of tights without ripping them. I don't think we can expect miracles in his deportment. And second, how many primary-school-aged girls have you seen acting like princesses?' Mum narrows her eyes at Dad – never a good sign.

'He's got to be girly enough that people believe he's a girl,' Dad protests.

'Yes, but he won't do that by sticking out like a sore thumb.' Mum looks over at me. 'Or a pink carnation – that dress has got to go. I'll find something a bit less . . . frilly.'

'Thanks, Mum.' I can't believe I'm grateful about the prospect of wearing a *less frilly dress*.

'But you've still got to do your best to be a convincing girl. That means no scratching, and no yanking at or laddering your tights.'

Mum's brand of tights must be a *lot* more comfortable than mine.

Mum turns to Dad. 'The cover story says that Josie's shy. That's what we should be concentrating on – if he can keep his mouth shut and stay in the background then he'll be fine.'

'You mean I shouldn't have a personality?'

Mum doesn't pick up my tone or is ignoring it. 'Right.'

Dad's paper-thin mobile warbles at him – he looks at it and then glances at Mum. 'Got to check the screens.'

By now I know that means he has to disappear into the secret spy room in the kitchen, the room I call Mission Control.

'Can I come?'

'No. You stay here and go over your cover with your mum. Don't want you slipping up on anything.'

'When am I going to get to see what you *do*?'

Dad makes a zipping gesture across his mouth. 'It's classified, I'm afraid.'

'So I'm stuck playing shy in a dress while you get to swan around doing *classified* stuff. Does that sound fair to you?'

Mum and Dad exchange a look.

'I suppose he should be a *little* familiar with what we do,' Mum says.

'Okay. I'll show you the room and the gadgets,' Dad says. 'But not until tomorrow – after school. When you've proved you're taking this seriously.'

It's not much, but it will have to do.

The next morning, Mum takes me to school. She's explained that our cover story is that we've relocated after both she and Dad found new jobs in the area. She's working part time as an interior designer for a chain of hotels, and Dad's in charge of checking security systems in shops and offices all over the region. It's a way they can keep moving to throw off the people trying to track them down and will make it easier to find out if they're still being followed. She reminds me for the billionth time that our enemies are looking for a family with a mum, dad and son so any slip-up on my part could lead to us being discovered. No pressure then.

'Once we're fairly sure we're not being watched, you can get the bus if you like,' Mum says as we park outside the small brick building. 'There's a service that goes from our village to this one.' She glances over at me. 'But maybe we should wait until you're confident about being able to keep your cover secure in all situations.'

She'll be waiting a long time. I haven't even worked out how to keep my wig secure in all situations.

Walking into the school with Mum feels like there's a spotlight on me with a sign over my head that spells out *FAKE GIRL*. This morning I tried again to convince them that girls wear trousers but even Mum agreed with Dad that I should stick with a skirt. Dad also made me wear an enormous pink smiley-faced butterfly clip in my wig. I'm doing my best to pretend it's not there. I wiggle my feet in the round-toed shoes, missing the soft give of my trainers, and take a breath as the receptionist shows us into the head's office.

'Hello, Josephine,' Mrs Harrison says, smiling. 'I really hope you'll enjoy being with us at Bothen Hill School.'

'Actually, we call her Josie,' Mum says.

Like that's so much better.

I stare at the floor as Mum talks to Mrs Harrison about me, explaining how shy I am, how I can't do any swimming because of my allergy to chlorine, how I prefer to keep quiet rather than join in activities. Josie sounds like the kind of person you'd want to stay a hundred miles away from.

I can't help thinking of Eddie – if I was at my old school now, we'd probably be whispering about the latest football match at the back of the class and getting told off by Mr Burnside. We'd be groaning about doing maths and literacy and kicking each other under the table. I'd give anything to be back with Eddie right now, even if it meant a whole day of doing decimals.

Instead, I'm trying to stop myself from scratching the tops of my legs. They're itching like crazy but Mum says if I ladder one more pair of tights I'll have to buy my own with my pocket money. And I really don't want to have to *pay* to be a girl.

'Well, I'm sure you need to be getting on so I'll take Josie down to Mr Caulfield's class. I know everyone will give her a warm welcome.' Mrs Harrison gives me what I'm pretty sure is a pitying smile.

'Good luck, darling,' Mum says. She waves and disappears out of the door. There she goes, off to drive ninety miles an hour to her next spy mission while I have to face Complete Humiliation in front of strangers. Thanks, Mum.

My palms are clammy as I follow Mrs Harrison down the corridor to my new classroom. She knocks and then leads me into the room towards Mr Caulfield at the front. He's got white hair and a beard and a round belly. I bet he gets asked to be Father Christmas at the school fair. I keep my eyes on him, avoiding looking at everyone else. My feet feel as if they've swollen to twice their size and my skin is hot. I realise that I don't have to act shy – I *am* shy.

'Hello, Josie, welcome to the Jackdaws class,' Mr Caulfield says as Mrs Harrison gives me a reassuring pat on the arm and leaves. 'Our classes are all named after birds – and since jackdaws make a right racket, it suits this class perfectly.'

Everyone laughs as Mr Caulfield leads me to a desk with an empty place. 'You can sit next to Sam.' Sam turns out to be the girl we saw when we arrived at the new house. The one who saw me in the pink dress. She gives me a now-you-see-it-now-you-don't smile and turns away. I can't blame her. I wouldn't want to make friends with someone with my dress sense either.

My knees look really knobbly now that I'm sitting down. I cover them with my hands. I don't think it's normal for a girl to have knees like a bag of marbles.

Mr Caulfield carries on with the lesson. The work is all right – it's pretty much what I was doing at my old school – but I miss having Eddie to nudge in the ribs and laugh with. Eddie wasn't exactly the perfect friend. He complained a lot and you couldn't rely on him to stick up for you if you got in trouble. And if you ever did something stupid he'd laugh at you for days. But still, he was my friend and having a friend is better than being alone.

At least that's what I think until break-time when

I'm in the playground and every girl in the class comes up to me and fires questions at me. Why don't they want to do something *normal* like have a game of football instead of standing around *chatting*?

'Do you like it here?'

'What was your old school like?'

'Why did you move?'

'Where do you live?'

'Where did you get your hair clip?'

I keep my answers short but I'm starting to panic. I'm supposed to keep in the background! I'm supposed to keep my wig straight and stay quiet! Luckily, my one-word answers make them lose interest in me and after a while I'm left by the side of the playground, watching people talk and play games.

I knew having spy parents would turn my life upside down, but I didn't think it would mean I'd be lonely.

I catch sight of Sam. She's playing football. She tries to take a shot at goal but she's tackled and the ball shoots over towards me. Automatically, I run forward and trap the ball with my foot. She looks a bit surprised but she gestures towards the goal. I take the shot and it goes in. Kicking the ball is the first natural thing I've done in days.

Sam whistles. 'Good goal.'

I can't stop myself grinning at her. 'Thanks.'

Then I remember – Josie's not supposed to be sporty. I have to get out of here before I do anything else to mess up my cover.

I hurry back to our block and down the corridor to the toilets. I have my hand on the door and I'm about to push through to the other side when a boy from my class stops and laughs.

'Where are you going?'

'What?'

I look up at the sign on the door I'd been about to go through – for the boys' toilets.

Well done, Josie. Two mistakes in less than a minute. I'm starting to understand how hard keeping up this cover is going to be.

'I wasn't going *in*, I just wanted to get something off my shoe,' I tell him. I lift up my foot, still leaning against the door, and brush something imaginary from it.

The boy keeps laughing. Which makes me want to do something I'm pretty sure isn't on Dad's list of Acceptable Girly Girl Behaviour.

'Leave her alone, Paul. She's only new.' Another boy is walking up to us.

Laughing Boy shrugs. He jams his hands in his pockets and wanders off.

'Ignore him,' says the boy. 'He's being stupid.'

'Thanks.'

'My name's Noah.'

'Right. I'm Joe . . . sie.'

'Yeah. Okay. Well, see you.' Noah swings off.

I sigh. When I was at my old school, I was never

interested in talking to the girls either.

I push into the girls' toilets. Luckily there's no one there. I lock myself into one of the cubicles. Maybe I can stay in here every break-time. Mum and Dad can come up with a reason for me having to shut myself away – some sort of illness, or a phobia. I could be frightened of any room that doesn't have a toilet in it.

I hear the door swing open, and then the sound of a girl's voice, and then another and another. In seconds it sounds like every single girl from the school has come in.

If I could flush myself down the toilet to get out of here, I would.

I'll have to brave it. Maybe I can sneak out and no one will take any notice. I open the cubicle and inch towards the door.

A football crowd of girls swivels round.

'There you are, Josie!' says one of the girls from the playground. 'We were worried about you.'

'It must be hard starting a new school,' says another.

'No . . . I'm fine.' I give a tiny smile and take another step towards the door.

Sam is with them. 'You live opposite me, don't you?'

'Yeah.'

'So you like football?'

I'm about to say no – I'm not supposed to like activities. 'Remember you're too shy to join in things,' Dad told me this morning. But Sam plays football. Sam might even like to talk about football. Can it really be that dangerous to be honest just once?

'Yeah, I love it.'

'Good.' She studies me. 'That was a nice goal in the playground. Maybe you can try out for the girls' team.'

'I don't know.' I can't tell her Mum and Dad are worried enough about the risk of me being discovered in PE lessons. I can't see them agreeing for me to do something sporty when I don't have to. Plus, it goes against the whole not-joining-in identity Josie's supposed to have. I'm not even allowed to ask anyone round to our house. But the thought of being able to play, even on a girls' team, is hard to resist.

'You really should,' Sam says. 'Jess has dropped out for the term because she broke her leg. We could do with someone who knows what they're doing.'

'Oi,' says a girl with dark hair tied back in a ponytail. 'You're not the only good player, you know.'

'I know. But we still need someone else on the team.' Sam turns to me. 'So will you come to the practice after school tomorrow?'

She looks so sure I'll agree that I find myself nodding.

Keeping out of things is harder than it sounds.

Chapter 6

'I don't know if you playing football is such a great idea,' Dad says when I tell Mum and Dad about Sam's invite.

'It's a *girls'* team. It's not like I'll be out of disguise.'

'But there are so many ways you could get found out. What about when you get changed? What if your wig falls off in a match?'

'I've got to handle all that for PE anyway. I'll pretend to be shy. I'll get changed in the loos. And Mum bought me a hairband and extra grips to help keep my wig on.'

'I don't know.' Dad rubs his chin where his beard used to be.

'I've had to move away from home, and all my friends. I have to dress up like a girl! You could at least let me join the school football team!'

Mum and Dad look at each other. Then I see Mum give an almost invisible shrug that means only one thing – victory.

'You'll have to be really, really careful,' Dad tells me.

'I will!'

Dad's about to say something else when they get one of those phone bleeps that means they have to disappear into Mission Control.

'I thought you were showing me the gadgets today?' I remind him.

Dad sighs. 'Yeah. But the job we're doing right now . . . well, it's tricky.'

Mum fishes in her purse and hands me a pound. 'Why don't you nip down to the shop at the corner? Buy yourself some chocolate. We should be done by the time you're back.'

'You're just trying to get rid of me,' I say, but I take the pound.

I nearly don't go to the shop. Mum hasn't had time to buy some other dresses yet so out of school I'm still stuck in the pink *thing* that Dad bought. But I decide I need chocolate more than dignity.

The woman behind the counter smiles at me when I come up. 'Hello, princess. What a pretty dress!'

Princess?! I drop my Maltesers on the counter and hand her my pound, restraining myself from throwing it at her.

'You're new round here, aren't you, love?'

Love?! 'We just moved.' My jaw's clenched so tight my teeth might crack.

'Here, you can have them as a welcome present,' she says, giving me back my money and then

64

pushing the chocolate over to me with a smile.

'Thanks,' I say, snatching up the chocolate from the counter. *Princess* and *love*! It's not even worth free chocolate.

I push my way out of the shop and slump down on the wall. The chocolate lasts about a second. I pull out my phone and play seven games of Mega Tank in a row to calm myself down but I can't even get past level one. If Eddie was here he'd be falling about. I've got disguise trauma!

'Mega Tank?' The voice makes me jump.

It's Sam. Uh oh. I stand up. Sam holds out her hand and I realise she wants to look at the phone. I give it to her, wishing I could think of a reason not to.

She swipes it to life, tapping at it expertly. 'Mega Tank, Dark Destroyer, Sonic Slicer . . . These are kind of boys' games, aren't they?'

'My dad put them on.'

'Doesn't he have his own phone?'

'He ran over it with his car.' Quick thinking isn't clever thinking. Why can't I keep my mouth shut?

'But there aren't any other games on here. You must like them too.'

My skin goes cold. But Dad's always said attack is the best line of defence. 'Why can't girls play those games?'

'Of course they can. It's just, with a phone like this – you know, really pink – and what you wear being so . . . so . . .'

We both look at my dress. It's hard not to see her point.

'But then you like football . . .' She shrugs. 'It's a bit funny, that's all.'

My stomach's doing flips – I keep hearing Dad in my head saying, 'This is serious.'

I reach out and take the phone back. '*You* like it too.'

'Yeah, but —'

'I'd better get back.' I've got to get out of here before I do something else that alerts her to the fact I am *not a normal girl.*

'Don't forget football tomorrow!' she calls after me as I set off for home.

As if. It's forgetting how to keep my cover in place that's the problem.

At home, Dad's finally ready to show me some of their gadgets.

'All right, look. I'm going to trust you.'

We're standing in front of the panel to Mission Control. He presses the code into the steel pad. I crane my neck so that I can memorise it. I figure it's good practice. Who knows, I might go into the spy business myself someday. Mr Burnside once said that kids often go into the same field as their parents. Back when Dad was supposed to be in politics and Mum was in computers, I wasn't that impressed. But growing up to be James Bond would be blinding. Especially in trousers.

The black panel at the back of the cupboard slides open. Dad gestures me in. 'Quickly.' The panel swishes shut behind us.

We've walked into a large room where every wall is covered with glowing blue screens. It's like the flight deck of a space ship. There are panels covered with buttons, and receivers set into the wall that look like a cross between a telephone and a walkie-talkie. There are slots for USB drives as well as for CDs and DVDs. Shelves on the right-hand side are crammed with techy-looking gear. It's a sweet shop of spy gadgets – and it's my mum and dad's office! Car chases are one thing but this room makes me realise that Mum and Dad are *proper* spies.

'Take a seat.' Dad points at one of the two swivel chairs and I sit down as he takes his position in front of the shelves. 'So. First you have your classic spy stationery,' he says. 'Cameras in pens, erasers, rulers, staplers.' He holds up a pencil sharpener. 'You can hide a camera in almost anything these days.'

I take one of the rulers and examine it, seeing

how the design incorporates a tiny eye and along the edge, a miniature button.

'Same goes for recording devices.' Dad shuffles through stuff on the next shelf and picks up some headphones. 'Mic in one ear and operating buttons in the other. Course, some are a bit more imaginative.' He roots around and holds up a bottle of Tipp-Ex. 'Unscrew the cap a little and it starts recording, screw it back down and it stops.'

'That's brilliant!' I could have had so much fun with that with Mr Burnside.

Dad pulls out a small black box. 'And this is one of my favourites.'

'What is it?'

'It's a disrupter.'

'A what?'

'A disrupter. Imagine you're after something, but there's a crowd around and you don't want witnesses. This creates a disruption for you wherever you set it, to distract attention from whatever you need to do.'

I wish Eddie and I had been able to get our hands on a disrupter. We could have *definitely* used it. 'What kind of disruption?'

'Oh, you can choose from a range. A little fire – controlled, of course – or a series of bangs that might be mistaken for gunshots or a car misfiring. Or fireworks – really small ones. Or an alarm – that kind of thing.' Dad pats it affectionately before putting it back.

I can't help staring as he rummages around on another shelf. I can't believe this gadget-wielding spy is my dad. He once killed our lawn mower by pouring oil in the petrol tank and now he knows how to operate miniature recording devices?

Dad smiles as if he's read my mind before carrying on with his demonstration. 'Then we have all the voice-activated recording equipment embedded in coins, pens, sunglasses ... and these are always useful, of course.' He holds up a handful of silver and gold watches.

'What, for when you're pretending to be selling Rolex knock-offs?'

'No. These all have double and triple functions – some are phones, some are recorders, some are detonators —'

'*Detonators?*'

Dad coughs. 'Yeah, I'll tell you about that another time.' He pulls out a little book. 'This is excellent.'

'A pocket diary?'

'Look.' Dad flips the pages until he gets to the end. Then, the whole book turns inside out and I can see a miniature keyboard and screen. 'Miniature laptop with untraceable internet access. Fantastic for hacking.' He picks up a thin, round silver case.

'What's that?'

'Your mum uses this all the time. Looks like a compact mirror – but it's actually a video-phone and camera. You press the buttons here to switch between the functions.'

He takes out more stuff as I try to imagine Mum

and Dad in action with it all, uncovering enemy secrets. It gives me an excited shivery feeling, like sitting in a dark cinema the moment before a film starts. I'm having to get to know my mum and dad all over again.

Dad goes on. 'Motion detector alarm clock, bugging devices in a mains adaptor, in a clothes hanger, in an egg timer, a paper clip, a packet of sugar. Here's a bionic ear for listening in to conversations up to a mile away. Always useful, that one. And here's another one of my favourites – internet dental floss.'

'What?' *Internet dental floss*? Even brushing my teeth could become a scene from a spy film!

Dad taps the box. 'Flip open the top and instead of dental floss you have a little wi-fi aerial. Lovely bit of kit.'

'And these keys?' I point to a bunch on the desk in front of me.

'They open things. *Anything*, in fact.' He picks up the keys and gives them a fond look. 'They can get you into any lock you want.'

'Any lock?' I hold out my hand and Dad lobs them over.

'Anything at all. If there's a lock on it, there's a key there to fit it.'

'And how about this?' Dad pulls a long, thin steel cable from the pile. He waves it at me. 'This is a version of what we used the other night. It latches onto a roof or window or whatever so you can climb out of sticky situations. It's military grade steel.'

I wonder how many times Dad's used it. It's weird to think of Mum and Dad as action heroes. Though considering what they've been making me do, 'heroes' might be a bit of an exaggeration.

Dad shows me how the pen cameras work and how they can be inserted into slots in the wall to transfer or print the digital images, and where recordings can be transferred onto memory sticks. As he's tapping screens and flicking buttons, I get an image of him as he used to be – spilling coffee in the car and making really bad dad jokes. Now he's showing me the tricks of the spy trade.

Grown-ups go on about how kids change so fast but no one ever talks about when *they* change overnight.

Dad pulls out a black sack. 'And this is essential.'

'What's in it?'

'Different characters.' He puts his hand in the sack and pulls out a pair of thick-rimmed glasses and pops them on his nose. Then he reaches back in and takes out a black hat, which he pulls down low over his forehead. Once more into the bag and this time it's a set of sideburns, which he sticks to his cheeks. He faces me. 'You see? I've become someone else.'

'No. You're Dad with a hat, glasses and bad facial hair.' I grin at him. The dad from our old life liked dressing up too. Maybe he hasn't changed as much as I thought. 'Everyone would know it's you if they looked hard enough,' I tell him.

'That's the point. Most people *don't* look hard

enough. Most people only see what they're looking for – if you give them something different, they simply won't recognise it.'

'No, sorry, don't know what you're talking about.'

'Look. Picture a friend in your mind.'

Weirdly, instead of Eddie, I think of Sam. I picture her short, spiky blond hair and her sharp right foot on the ball. 'Okay. Now what?'

'If you look for him in the street you know what you'll be looking for, right?'

'Well, yeah . . .'

'But if someone who's a lot taller than him with a different hair colour walks by, will you think it's him?'

'No, course not.'

'But it *could* be. Your friend could dye his hair, put on some heeled shoes, and you wouldn't even glance at him because he *wouldn't be what you were expecting to see.*'

This does explain why I haven't been immediately sussed out as a Not Very Believable Girl. And maybe it's also why I never suspected my parents weren't what they said they were for all those years. I think of how many secrets they've kept from me and how much I have left to find out.

'All you have to remember is that people don't notice half as much as you think. Unless they're a spy, of course.' Dad smiles and picks up a bag from the bottom shelf. 'What do you think of this?' Dad delves into the bag and then throws a football at me.

I catch it and weigh it in my hands. It's amazing quality – the kind of ball that professionals play with – heavy and solid. 'It's a beauty.'

'It's yours. Hope it brings you luck when you try out for the team.'

'Thanks!' There's a seam in one side that's thicker than the rest. I bring it close to my face to examine it.

'Keep talking,' Dad tells me, and reaches out to touch the side of the ball.

'I don't understand. Isn't it a normal football?'

'That's enough.'

Dad presses the ball again, and my voice comes out. 'I don't understand. Isn't it a normal football?'

'It's a recorder?'

'Yeah. But it's also a high-class bit of football kit – the sound equipment is encased in steel so you can whack the ball as hard as you like without worrying about damaging the recorder. I wanted to give you something to make up for all this stuff going on. And maybe it will come in useful sometime.'

'Uh . . . and why would a recording football be useful?'

'Trust me. You never know.' Dad shows me where the almost invisible buttons are, just inside the seam. 'Simple to use, too. Press once to record, press again to stop, press the other button to play it back.'

It really *is* a blinding football. 'Thanks, Dad.'

'No problem. I know it's hard on you, all this.'

Tell me about it. I don't just deserve a football, I deserve a medal.

Chapter 7

The next morning, Mum draws up in front of the school without turning off the engine. She checks her rear-view mirror, then reaches over me to pop open the glove compartment. Inside, a slim steel box with a row of tiny green lights is whirring softly. Mum glances at it, then clicks the compartment shut.

'What does that do?' I ask her.

She smiles as she pulls my bag from the back seat and hands it to me. 'Satellite technology. It tracks people and cars in the surrounding area and analyses patterns of movement so we can pick up on any unusual behaviour.'

'You mean, like people following us.'

'Exactly. You have to be on your guard – especially when you're following your normal routines. That's when you're most at risk. Now, off you go.'

I look at the clock on the dashboard. 'Registration's not for ten minutes.'

'So?'

'So that's ten extra minutes for me to risk blowing my cover.' After my conversation with Sam yesterday, I figure I should cut down the amount of time I have to talk to anyone.

'I've got things to do,' Mum says. 'Besides, you need to become confident with your new identity.' She pats my knee. 'Don't worry, it'll get easier.'

Grown-ups always say this. I think they forget that the amount of time needed for something to get easier is the time it takes for you to become so ancient you've forgotten how hard things can be.

'Now, do you have the headband and grips to keep your wig on during football?'

'Yes.'

'Excellent. Good luck, sweetheart. We'll see you later.'

I get out of the car and trudge towards the school. I'm pretty sure I know what prisoners feel like when they go to jail.

'Hey, Josie!' A girl from my class rushes up to me as I push through the gate. 'I'm Melissa, I sit behind you.'

'Hi.' I flash her my best 'shy smile' and tip my head so that my wig hair falls across my face. I have to admit, long hair does have its uses.

'A few of us are meeting in the hall at lunchbreak. Why don't you come too?'

'Um . . .' Stress freezes my brain. I know I need to find a reason not to say yes. I know the same way birds sense a cat creeping up behind them in the garden.

'You must be really lonely after leaving your old school. Did you have lots of friends there?'

I keep my head down and mutter. 'Don't know. Not really.'

'You've got to come then. Everyone's really nice. We're doing something really good. You'll love it.' Melissa waves at someone across the playground. 'I'll come and find you after lunch.'

She's off before I can think of an excuse, or can break one of my own legs. I'll have to talk to Mum and Dad. I don't think they know what girls are like about getting you to join in with things. I remember Eddie saying that when his sister Tilly was younger, she held people hostage in her room and forced them to have tea with her teddies. I wish I could tell him that I understand what he was talking about now.

Mr Caulfield is halfway through the morning literacy lesson on metaphors and similes (I hate being a girl like a football player hates an own goal) when Mrs Harrison pops her head round the door.

'Sorry to disturb you,' she says. 'I just wanted to give you those files you asked for.'

Mr Caulfield hurries over and takes a large yellow folder from her. He looks as if she's told him he's won the lottery. 'I'm so grateful to you for offering to do this,' Mrs Harrison says. 'We're having a nightmare finding a good accountant.'

Mr Caulfield smiles. 'It's no trouble. I want to do as much as I can for the school before I retire.'

For someone who's taken on extra work, Mr Caulfield looks really happy about it. But maybe he's not thinking about the work, maybe he's thinking about his retirement. I really hope by the time Mr Caulfield leaves, I'll be long gone and back to being myself again and away from all these girls. Three to six months, Dad said. And to use another simile, maybe, like a good prisoner, I might even get out early on good behaviour. The thought makes me smile.

I eat my sandwiches quickly and slip out of the side door into the playground, planning to head for the toilets again. This time I just won't come out of the cubicle. But as I'm heading towards our block, a hand grabs my elbow.

'There you are!' Melissa tugs at me. 'Come on, it's this way.' She keeps her hand tight on my arm the whole way to the hall – like a hooked fish, I have absolutely no chance of escaping.

There are two other girls waiting for us. One is fiddling with an iPod dock and the other one is standing in a pose like she's on a magazine cover.

'That's Nerida and Suzy,' says Melissa. The girls wave at me.

'We're doing a dance routine for the end of term Achievers' Assembly,' Melissa says. 'You can learn it with us.'

'A dance?' My chest tightens and my breath catches in my throat.

Melissa doesn't notice that I'm becoming *very ill*. 'Don't worry, it's really easy. Watch us first and then you can join in.' Join in? I'm more likely to pass out!

The girl called Nerida presses *Play* and some boy-band song blasts out. The three girls wiggle around the room like eels, waving their arms in the air and grinning as if they've just been given tickets to the Cup final.

I take a step backwards towards the door, staring in horror as they put their hands on their hips and circle them round and round. How do they even *do* that? I'm not convinced that girls are completely human.

Nerida and Suzy waggle their fingers as if they're stroking an invisible cat – lots of invisible cats. Melissa puts her hands behind her back and sways from side to side. Maybe she's got an itch in a hard-to-reach place. When they see me staring they erupt into giggles. I have no idea what they think is so funny but they're hurting my ears.

Melissa kind of shimmies over to me and grabs my hand. 'Come on, Josie, it's easy!' She pulls me across the floor.

'NOOOO!'

Melissa drops my hand. 'What's the matter?'

They stare at me as the song comes to an end.

'I . . . um . . . I have a bruise. Where you touched me.' I pull my sleeve down.

'Oh, sorry.'

Maybe if I wish really, really hard, the ground will open up and they will VANISH.

Luckily, the bell goes before I can do anything else to get myself in trouble.

'Don't worry,' Melissa says, 'there's lots of time to learn the dance.'

'I don't think I can. I've got, um, problems with my arches.'

'Oh.' Melissa sounds disappointed. She wouldn't be if she could see me dance.

In the playground, Sam catches up with me as I'm walking back. 'I saw you come out with Melissa

85

and her gang. So, you like dancing?'

Before I can stop myself, the words burst out, 'I hate it!'

She looks a bit surprised. 'Oh. Well, football practice is only a few hours away. You'll enjoy that.'

'Yeah.' I decide to keep my head down for the afternoon. I've got to learn how to keep my mouth shut.

My football kit isn't perfect – it's *light years* away from perfect. The tracksuit bottoms are baggy and have way too many flowers on them. But at least it isn't a dress. As soon as the bell goes, I lock myself in the toilets to get changed and make sure my headband and grips are securely in place. I don't need any more disguise slip-ups today. I drop my kit bag at the edge of the playground and bounce the football Dad gave me as I walk towards Sam and the others. I almost – *almost* – feel all right.

'Nice ball,' Sam says, 'but we're only supposed

to use the school kit.' Then Sam takes the ball from me and grins. 'Mr Caulfield is still getting the cones for practice, though, so let's give it a quick go.' She flicks the ball up onto her chest then lets it drop to the ground, resting her right foot on top of it. 'Ready?'

I fix my eyes on the ball. 'Go.'

Sam heads towards the net with a clean kick. I hold back a bit, not wanting to embarrass her straightaway.

She scores a perfect goal.

Fluke.

Sam retrieves the ball and when I try to tackle her, easily sidesteps me.

Another goal.

Another fluke.

Next time, I go after her the same way I'd have gone after Eddie. I manage to get the ball from her for a second before Sam reclaims it.

Another goal.

What is *going on*?!

Mr Caulfield appears and blows

a whistle. Sam passes me the ball and we walk towards him. 'Good shots,' I tell her, trying not to sound shocked.

'Good tackling.'

For a second I think she's making fun of me, the way Eddie would have done, and then I realise she's serious. 'Thanks.'

'Hello, Josie, I'm glad you've decided to join us.' Mr Caulfield points at my ball. 'But didn't anyone tell you you're only allowed to use school equipment?'

'Sorry, I just really wanted to try it out.'

'That's all right. But I'm afraid I'll have to confiscate it until practice is over.' He holds his hands out and I reluctantly pass it over. 'I just have to make a quick call so you lot go ahead and get yourselves warmed up.'

By the time we've done a few stretches and laps around the pitch, Mr Caulfield's back and proper play gets underway. About halfway through the practice I realise that I'm getting a better game as Josie than I ever did as Joe. I've had more time on the ball than any match I've ever played – the girls are great about passing – and my side wins! It's blinding! At the end, Mr Caulfield gives me my ball back and Sam and I talk football while we wait to be picked up at the gate.

I'm planning to tell Mum all about it, but as soon as I get in the car she puts her finger to her lips. 'Sorry, sweetheart. I'm waiting for a call from HQ – can we chat later?'

'Oh, okay.' I guess it's natural that in our new life, spy stuff comes first and my stuff comes second, but that doesn't mean it's easy.

Mum pats my hand and pulls out onto the road. 'It's such a relief that we've been able to tell you the truth about what we do. It's good to know you understand we can't always give you as much attention as before.'

Then Mum's hands-free phone rings and she's talking in code about mission this and mission that while I stare out of the window. When I imagined living the life of Dan McGuire, this isn't exactly what I had in mind.

* * *

When we get home, Dad tells me my dinner is on a plate in the fridge and to microwave it when I'm hungry. Then he and Mum disappear into Mission Control.

You'd think having spies for parents would be non-stop excitement. You'd think I'd be learning about code-breaking and computer hacking and catching villains.

You'd be wrong.

Up in my room, I'm practising spinning the football on my finger when I touch the *Play* switch by mistake. Mr Caulfield's voice is loud and clear. 'Now we've got the files you can transfer the funds. I'll let you know when the grant money comes into the school and then you can put that into my account as well.'

There's a pause as a distant, muffled voice says something. Then it's back to Mr Caulfield. 'Look, by the time Mrs Harrison realises, I'll have taken my early retirement and be long gone. You do your bit and I'll do mine. Okay?'

A phone clatters onto a receiver and that's it – there's nothing else on the recording.

Mr Caulfield must have activated the recording device when he took the ball into school during football practice. But why was he having a conversation about putting school money into his own bank account? I suppose it must be something to do with him doing that accounting work for Mrs Harrison. He's not exactly the criminal type. People who look like Father Christmas don't commit crimes.

But the recording gives me an idea – if Mum and Dad won't train me to be a spy, maybe I can train myself. And I think I've found a perfect first practice case.

Chapter 8

Family breakfasts just aren't the same these days. Dad used to make porridge or boiled eggs, Mum would make tea and toast and we'd all sit round quietly, maybe with them asking me a couple of questions about school and me grunting into my bowl until they told me to hurry up or I'd be late. Like a normal family.

Not any more.

Now Mum or Dad rush around garbling code words, or one of them disappears off into Mission Control, or sits hunched over a laptop, peering at the screen, or punches numbers into their phone, or goes off in the car on some secret errand. Or sometimes Mum is in a corner of the room talking into her spy compact. And now that I take the bus with Sam, I don't even see them on the way to and from school. It's as if telling me the truth has given them a Licence to Ignore their son. But at least I can get on with my investigation in peace.

While I eat breakfast I decide on a plan. My football recording is going to be the basis for my first spy mission. It doesn't matter if it turns out that Mr Caulfield isn't doing anything wrong as long as I learn how to be a good spy. Then maybe I can convince Mum and Dad to let me help them on one of their missions – or at least give me proper training.

First of all I need to borrow some of Mum and Dad's equipment. When Dad nips upstairs for his shower and Mum's gone off for her latest appointment, I punch the code into the pad and slip inside Mission Control. I grab a selection of spy gear and I'm out again in seconds. I have just enough time to pile it all in my rucksack before having to meet Sam at the bus stop.

We talk about football all the way. Sam even likes Santos! When I'm talking to her, I almost forget who I am – or who I'm supposed to be.

But when I see Melissa in the playground, it all comes back with a sinking-stomach rush.

'Hi, Josie! Here.' She hands me an envelope and smiles. 'My birthday party's tomorrow after school. I'd really like you to come.'

'Um, thanks.' She's wearing a hair slide with a pink butterfly on it that's a lot like mine so I guess she's forgiven me for not joining in the dancing. I can take being friends with Sam – she's normal! She likes football! But Melissa looks like the kind of girly girl Dad wants me to be. It's a bit too close for comfort.

I follow Sam into our block and we hang up our coats. Dad's insisted I wear the one he bought – it's dark pink with sequins on the collar. I sigh as I watch Sam put her dark blue jacket on the hook.

'So, are you going?' Sam nods at the envelope from Melissa.

'Uh, maybe.' No chance. I just need to come up with the excuse. Mum and Dad said I should keep to myself so they'll be happy for me not to go. I'll be spared Melissa and her balloon animals – or whatever she's having at her party.

I concentrate on keeping an eye on Mr Caulfield during literacy and maths. He keeps nipping out to get things he's forgotten – paper, Tipp-Ex, a new pad of paper. It's probably because he's getting old and losing his memory but I have to think with a spy brain – he *could* be making more phone calls. The only way to find out is to plant some recording equipment on him.

I've just got to figure out how.

After break, we go to the leisure centre for swimming. I sit next to Sam on the bus and she tells me how she learned to swim when her mum took her to Greece.

'It was so warm and there were fish everywhere. It was like swimming in an aquarium.'

'You're lucky,' I tell her. 'I learned in a pool down the road from where we used to live. Once I saw an old man blow his nose in the shallow end and my mum still wouldn't let me get out!'

Sam laughs. Then she frowns – just as I realise what I've said. 'But I thought Mr Caulfield said you were allergic to chlorine. Isn't that why you're not swimming today?'

Mum and Dad should have sewn my mouth shut.

'Yeah, but . . . the pool I was talking about didn't have any chlorine in it. It was a special pool.'

'But you told me you're afraid of water as well.'

'It was ages ago,' I say quickly. 'Before I was afraid. Or allergic.'

'Oh.' Sam has *I'm not sure I believe you* written all over her face. I can see she's working up to another question, and decide to get in there first.

'When's Mr Caulfield retiring?'

'Next summer. I think that's what my mum said. We'll have Mr Sentance in September.'

'Oh, right, of course. I heard him talking about it, that's all.' I know from Dan McGuire how important it is to collect background information on your subject. I guess next summer is what Mr Caulfield meant by early retirement.

When we walk into the centre, Mr Caulfield sends everyone off to get changed. I wait, wondering where to go and wishing I could follow the rest of the boys. Just the smell of chlorine makes me want to do a cannonball into the water.

'Go through the changing rooms, Josie, and then you can sit and read in the gallery on the other side.'

Walk through the girls' changing rooms? Is he joking? 'Isn't there another way?'

Mr Caulfield looks surprised.
'I don't think so. Anyway,
I'd prefer you to stick
with the other girls, okay?'

No. It's not okay at all.

I take a deep breath and keep my eyes down –
but that doesn't stop me hearing things.

'My bra straps are killing me,' Nerida says.

I speed up but because
I've got my eyes on the
floor I nearly walk right into
Melissa.

'Do *you* wear a bra,
Josie?'

'YOU HAVE GOT TO BE JOKING!'

Everyone stares at me.

Mum and Dad might be spies, but I don't think
they have a clue how stressful this undercover
stuff is.

Being in the gallery during the swimming session
makes me think of our old life. I used to love
swimming. Eddie liked playing this game called
submarines. One person was the submarine and
one person was the missile. You took it in turns to
be the missile and try to sink the submarine. The
only problem was that Eddie was a lot bigger than

me and so he was a lot better at being the missile. By the end of the game, I'd be half drowned. But most of the time swimming was a laugh, though if it was with school we always ended up getting shouted at by Mr Burnside. Mr Burnside wasn't a fan of submarines.

I've brought my favourite Dan McGuire book, *Dan McGuire and the Code-Cracker*, but it's hard to concentrate when everyone else is splashing about and laughing. Then Mr Caulfield sits a couple of rows in front of me. I forget all about the swimming session and the book because Mr Caulfield has his mobile in his hand. This is my chance to do a secret recording!

I inch my leg over the seat in front of me so that I can drop into the row directly behind him. He doesn't notice me. He's already talking by the time I'm in earshot. I click on my recording pen and hold it out as far as I can. His conversation might turn out to be boring but at least I'll be getting some practice in.

'I've had an excellent idea of how to add to our

takings . . . a little charity work project. It will mean we have to move quickly – but I think it could improve both our bank balances. There's only so much money to be gained from the local council's grants, after all.'

There's a pause as Mr Caulfield listens.

'Mark, Mark, you worry too much. You forget that I've been at Bothen Hill School for fifteen years – why would anyone suspect me? I'm just making sure my bank balance will be big enough for me to live on when I retire.'

Not so boring after all.

The leisure centre's swimming instructor blows a whistle and everyone swims back to the end of the pool. I quickly pull out my book and bury myself in the pages as Mr Caulfield says goodbye and pockets his mobile.

'Josie!'

I pretend to be lost in my book and only react after a second. 'Oh, hello, Mr Caulfield.'

'I didn't see you there.' Mr Caulfield's smile doesn't quite reach his eyes.

'I came back from the toilet and then got into my book, sir.'

'You like to under-line your favourite bits, do you?' Mr Caulfield nods at the recording pen still in my hand.

'Yeah.'

I must sound convincing. Mr Caulfield relaxes. 'Well, I'm glad you found a way to pass the time, Josie, well done.'

I've definitely found a way to pass the time. Spying on Mr Caulfield looks as if it might prove to be a proper mission after all.

Chapter 9

Mum picks up a piece of microfilm with some tweezers and carefully puts it on the top right-hand corner of an envelope. Then she peels off a stamp and sticks it down on top of the film. I'm getting used to this kind of thing now. It's almost like watching her doing the ironing. Mum hands the envelope over to Dad and then looks at me. 'Well, I think you should go.'

'What? You said I should keep in the background! You said I shouldn't join in things!'

'Yes, but then you decided to join the football team,' says Mum. 'So that's changed your cover identity already, hasn't it?'

'And you say this Melissa is "girly" so I think it's an excellent idea for you to be friends with her. It will make you more believable.' Dad addresses the envelope with his left hand, which turns his handwriting into an almost illegible scrawl.

'No, it will make me more miserable.'

'It's a birthday party. What's not to like?' Mum looks at my face. 'Don't answer that.'

After school, Melissa's mum picks up everyone who's going to the party. On the way to Melissa's house, I pretend to laugh whenever they do, even though I don't really understand what they're laughing about. Eddie's mum had a friend from France who used to come and stay with them. They'd speak French really fast and when I was over at Eddie's, I'd feel really embarrassed to hear them, as if I should know what they were saying.

I feel the same way now – and they're talking English!

We arrive at Melissa's house and go into the living room. 'Surprise!' Melissa throws out her arms. 'Pamper party!'

I have no idea what a pamper party is but it takes about three seconds to guess. Every surface is covered with make-up, hairbrushes, sparkly hair clips and some steel roddy-type things with plugs. It's detention with torture.

'Who's up for the first makeover?'

I can't help it. I make a squeaking sound.

'Are you all right, Josie?'

'Can I have a drink of water?'

'Of course, help yourself.' Melissa's mum smiles at me. 'I'm so looking forward to doing your hair, Josie, it's so pretty.'

You're not laying a finger on me, Mrs.

Sam follows me into the kitchen. 'Are you okay?'

I gulp down a glass of water. And then another one. And then another one. Problem solved – I'll stay in the toilet for the entire party!

'Yeah, sure,' I say. I just need to come up with a reason why no one can touch my face or my head.

I go back into the living room and up to Melissa's mum. She's busy putting dark blue stuff on Nerida's eyelids with a plastic stick.

'How do I look?' Nerida grins up at me.

'Nice.' If you like pandas.

'I'll be able to do you in a minute, Josie,' Melissa's mum says.

'That's okay. Actually, I'm a bit allergic, so I'll just watch.'

'Oh dear – I'm sorry. But even if you can't have make-up on, I can still give you a nice hair-do.'

'No!'

Melissa's mum holds her stick in mid-air and looks at me.

'I mean, my head is really sensitive.'

Sam snorts.

'I see.' Melissa's mum shoots a look at Melissa. You can see she's thinking, *Who is this weird girl?*

'I know!' Melissa grabs a nail file and waves it at me like a knife. 'Mum can do your nails!'

'Oh, no, I —'

'Come on, Josie, it'll be great!'

Melissa drags me over to the sofa and pushes me down so that I'm sitting in front of her mum. Melissa's mum finishes off Nerida's face by smearing her lips in bright pink goo and then leans over and grabs one of my hands. 'You're going to love this.'

I'm really not.

She files my nails into points like a cat. Great, now I have claws. Then she paints them with purple, foul-smelling glossy paint. Just when I think the agony is over, she decides to stick little sparkly stickers, all different shades of pink, on each nail. My hands have been turned into finger puppets!

'There. Isn't that lovely?' Melissa's mum asks proudly.

Melissa, Nerida and Suzy coo over my hands like they're kittens.

I have to get out of here.

'I'm just going to get some more water,' I say, getting up from the sofa and backing towards the kitchen.

'I'll come too,' Sam says. 'I'm not bothered about getting a makeover.'

Wait, it's that easy? Why didn't I say that?

'Well, there are some craft-making things in the kitchen,' Melissa's mum says. 'I was planning on that for later, but you could start now if you don't want to have your face and hair done.'

'Great!' I sound extra enthusiastic to balance things out.

We find blank cards, pens, glue and about a thousand pots of glitter on the table. I sink into one of the chairs and pick up a pen. What would a girl draw? A puppy? A bunch of flowers? A baby? A baby with a puppy and a bunch of flowers?

Then I see Sam is drawing a football strip – Santos's football strip!

I feel like Dan McGuire when he's pulled out of quicksand in *Dan McGuire and the Dunes of Doom.*

'Hey, that's good.'

'It'll be even better with glitter.' Sam picks up the glue pen.

If she can do it, so can I.

I set to work, dividing my card into squares and drawing the strip of every first-division team. It turns out football strips look blinding in glitter.

By the time the rest of the girls come through, Sam and I have almost finished. It's a shame really – making cards is actually not a bad way to spend an afternoon.

'Lovely work, girls. Now how about some tea?'

Tea is basically the same as any other birthday tea – the same sandwiches (pointless), same crisps, same carrot sticks (also pointless), same orange and blackcurrant squash. But Melissa's birthday cake is in the shape of a microphone and is covered with pink icing. 'For my little star,' her mum says.

After tea, Melissa gets all bouncy and giggly. She drags us into the living room and runs to the corner where a black box and a microphone have appeared. 'Second surprise! We're doing karaoke!'

Everyone else laughs and grabs the song lists from Melissa's mum. Nerida's already doing that circle thing with her hips.

I take a step back towards the kitchen. 'I can't do it.' I'm hoping Sam will agree with me and suggest doing more glitter football strips. But she doesn't.

'Come on, Josie,' she says, 'you can't be allergic to singing.'

'I'm not a very good singer.'

'Neither am I. It doesn't matter. It's just about having a laugh.' Sam gives me an odd look and I realise I have to go along with it so that she doesn't get suspicious.

From this point on, things get hazy – like a

nightmare when you skip from scene to scene. Melissa sings something that has 'Ooo baby, baby' in it over and over again. Then Nerida sings something by Lady Gaga and Sam sings something I've never heard of but involves her making sounds like dolphins calling each other in the wild. Then they're pushing me to the front and 'Mamma Mia' by Abba is blaring out. Abba! Eddie used to make fun of the girls for singing Abba in the playground after they'd all seen some film. I can just picture him, his hand over his mouth, bent over with laughter.

Nerida puts her arm round me and bumps her hip against mine. I croak out the words that are projected on the wall. I can hear my voice echoing in the mic. I sound like a sick frog. The other girls flick their hair around and bounce up and down on their feet. Melissa's mum is taking photos on her digital camera and she's promising to email copies to us.

Photos! Great. This isn't just the Afternoon of Shame, it could also put my identity at risk! Mum and Dad had better be ready to help destroy the evidence. This afternoon is completely their fault.

After Mum picks me up I refuse to speak to her for the rest of the evening. There's only one answer to her earlier question of 'What's not to like?'

Everything.

For the next few days I try to distract myself from the memories of Melissa's party and the nightmares I have about being smothered in pink lip gloss and being forced to sing at a school assembly – alone. I put all my energy into spying on Mr Caulfield. I re-read my Dan McGuire books for tips, and make notes on what I find out about Mr Caulfield as soon as I get home. I search his desk at break-time after I spill my pencil case on the floor accidently-on-purpose, and learn that:

- Mr Caulfield has a habit of putting his coffee cup down on his lesson plans.
- Mr Caulfield likes gardening. Evidence: a pile of seed packets in his drawer for tomatoes, carrots, spring onions, peas and cress.
- Mr Caulfield reads *Model Engineer*, *Model Boats* and *Gardeners' World Magazine*.

It's not exactly the kind of high crime material I've been hoping for. After that promising conversation at the swimming pool, Mr Caulfield is turning out to be just another ordinary teacher.

But Dan McGuire never gives up, so neither will I.

Chapter 10

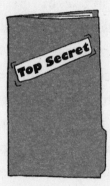

When I come down to the kitchen on Friday morning, Mum is sitting at the table, surrounded by piles of paper with black lines blocking out most of the text.

'What's all this then?' I pick up one of the pieces of paper.

Mum snatches it out of my hand. 'Never you mind. Go and get your cornflakes – you'll have to eat them in the living room.'

'Why can't I eat them at the table?'

'I can't afford to take a chance of you seeing something you shouldn't.'

I don't point out that since I don't have x-ray vision, that doesn't seem very likely. She's got her Serious Spy look on and I know not to question it. Really, there's no difference between her new Serious Spy look and her old Furious Mum expression. I get my bowl of cereal and go and sit on the sofa.

I bet most people don't have to worry about causing some kind of international crisis by eating their cornflakes in the wrong place. It's getting to be more and more important to prove to Mum and Dad that I'm up to being a proper spy.

So when Mum goes upstairs to get dressed, I nip into Mission Control to raid it again. Luckily, the one thing about Dad that has definitely not changed is that he leaves things in a mess. The spy gadgets are still in a jumble from when he was showing them to me – there's no way they'll notice anything's missing.

At lunchtime I make my way to the car park next to the playground. I've already waited to see Mr Caulfield arrive in his car, so I know he drives a blue Vauxhall Astra. We're not supposed to go into the car park but there's a small side gate to it from the playground and I slip through it when no one is looking. I scoot down and run to the car, peering in the window. On the back seat is a dark blue bag with the logo *Bothen Hill News* on it.

I look over my shoulder – no one's around – and I click the multi-remote I borrowed from Mission Control. There's a loud bleep as the doors unlock. I wait a second and then pull the back door open.

I slip a voice-activated recording ruler on the floor under the passenger seat and then inch the bag open. I get a glimpse of a thick wodge of papers and a folder that says *ATTN: Mark Rial*.

Mr Caulfield was talking to someone called

Mark on the recording I made at the leisure centre! I know from Dan McGuire that you should keep infiltration time to a minimum so I'll have to make a separate plan for looking at the papers.

I click the door shut and relock the car, then run to the side gate and slip back into the playground. I've pulled my football out of my bag – if anyone's seen me come in I'll say I kicked my ball into the car park by accident.

I dribble the ball away from the gate and then lob it against the wall. Before I can get to it, Sam's run up and kicked it up onto her chest. She holds it in front of her. 'This really is a great ball.'

'Yeah, thanks.' I hold out my hands for it.

But Sam's spun it round and is examining it. 'Is this a faulty seam?' She peers closely at the part where the recording controls are.

'No. I mean, yes.'

'There's a funny little dent here . . .'

I reach out for it but it's too late – we're listening to the recording of Mr Caulfield's conversation.

I grab the ball and scrabble to find the off button

– but not before Sam's heard the whole thing.

Sam looks at me as if I'm off my rocker. 'I don't get it. You've got a football recorder and you recorded Mr Caulfield?'

'It was by accident – when he confiscated my ball.'

'But why have you got a *recording football*?'

I wish I could tell Sam the truth – all of it. She's been the one person who's made school bearable. But Dan McGuire's first rule is 'Trust no one' and if she lets something slip, I could put my whole family in danger. I decide on a half-truth.

'Do you know the Dan McGuire books?'

'Sure. I got the box set for Christmas.'

'You did?'

Eddie was never interested in Dan McGuire. He thought reading was boring. So Sam liking him as well is totally blinding. I'm about to ask her what her favourite book is when she taps my football.

'So? What's that got to do with you having recording equipment?'

'Oh. Well. Yeah. I read them all the time. So my mum and dad have always given me presents to do with spies.'

'Like this ball?'

'Yeah. Lots of stuff like that. And I heard this conversation and thought I'd practise my spying skills by checking it out.'

'That recording must be to do with Mr Caulfield doing the accounts for school,' Sam says. 'I remember my mum said how nice he was for offering. She says doing the accounts for anything is a real pain.'

'I know it doesn't sound likely, but I don't think he was being nice.' I take out the recording pen and play her the conversation from the swimming pool. It's a bit harder to hear him on that one because of all the background splashing but you can get the gist. 'You see what I mean? It's a bit suspicious.'

'Maybe, but my mum's a reporter,' Sam tells me, 'and she always says you have to have *loads* of evidence before you can prove something.'

'Do you want to help me see if there is any?' It's risky involving Sam but I'm tired of being on my own all the time. Besides, now that she knows about the gadgets, it'll be hard to hide what I'm doing from her in any case.

Sam shakes her head. 'I can't believe Mr Caulfield would do anything wrong. He doesn't even look like a criminal.'

'I know – but the best ones never do.' In the True Stories section of *Dan McGuire and the Acid Armour*, there's a bit about a spy called James Rivington who ran a coffee shop. Would you suspect the person who sold you a latte?

Sam hesitates for a second. 'And you have lots of spy equipment?'

'Loads.' At least I don't have to lie about that.

'I guess it would be fun to do a bit of proper spying,' she says. 'But it doesn't mean I think he's guilty.'

'Great.' Even if I can't tell her all my secrets, it's a relief to be able to share my mission with Sam. What's the fun of having genius gadgets if you have to do the investigation alone?

For someone who isn't even sure if Mr Caulfield is guilty or not, Sam really gets into the whole spy mission idea. She says we should call it Operation Numbered because if I'm right about Mr Caulfield committing a crime then his teaching days are numbered. 'And,' she says, 'we might get a supply teacher in for the rest of term – and they *never* set homework!'

On the bus home, I tell Sam about the recording ruler and the bag in the back of Mr Caulfield's car with the papers I saw.

'We could do a bag swap so we can take photos of whatever's in there. You've got a camera, right?'

'Yeah, but how do we get another *Bothen Hill News* bag?'

Sam laughs. 'Easy. They gave out loads of them to promote the paper. I told you. My mum's a reporter – she *works* for *Bothen Hill News*. We've got about ten of them at home.'

'Brilliant!'

By the time we reach my house we've worked out the details of the first stage of Operation Numbered. 'Do you want me to come in so we can make some more plans?' asks Sam.

'Uh, no, better not. I'm not allowed to bring anyone home without telling my parents first.' I'm not allowed to bring anyone home at all – and this is the first time I've minded.

'Can't you just run in and tell them now?'

'No, they work really hard and they get . . . really tired so they like to know, you know, way in advance.' If I was Pinocchio, my nose would be in Australia by now.

'I see,' Sam says. She glances up at my house and then back at me with an odd look on her face.

It's definitely time to change the subject. 'So is your dad a reporter as well?'

'No. It's just me and my mum – my dad left ages ago. Anyway, I'll go home and dig out one of those bags ready for Monday.'

'Great. And, uh, maybe you can come round another time.' My Pinocchio nose has made it to New Zealand.

It's hard not to think about how much easier life would be if Mum and Dad *weren't* undercover spies.

Chapter 11

At the end of assembly on Monday, Mrs Harrison makes an announcement.

'I'm sure we're all aware of how well our girls' football team has been doing in the school league tables. As you may know, our next match will be between our own team here at Bothen Hill and the girls at St Colmer's. But Mr Caulfield has managed to arrange something rather exciting.

The game will take place at the local *professional* football pitch!'

An excited murmur starts up. 'And this won't be just any game. A local journalist has agreed to cover the match!'

'That'll be my mum!' Sam whispers to me.

Mrs Harrison holds up her hand for quiet. 'The reason for this is that we will be raising money and awareness for a very worthy cause that Mr Caulfield has brought to our attention – the charity Start Sports. As you know, we usually support the charities Water Aid and Oxfam with our school events, but this term we are happy to give our fund-raising power to a new charity that is clearly very dear to Mr Caulfield. So I hope everyone here will do their bit to contribute to this exciting project – whether it's by playing on the team, collecting donations or getting your friends and family to come along.'

I've got two thoughts in my head.

1. If this is anything to do with that conversation of Mr Caulfield's and it turns out he's doing

something criminal with this charity, then I now officially hate Mr Caulfield.

2. A chance to play on a professional football pitch! Covered by a real journalist! I love Mr Caulfield!

The bell rings and everyone files out. Melissa and Nerida are already talking about getting their picture in the local paper.

As soon as we're in the corridor, Sam nudges me. 'Come to the toilets.'

'Why?'

'Because it's a good place to talk, idiot.'

That's one mystery cleared up.

In the toilets, Sam checks all the cubicles before speaking. 'Didn't Mr Caulfield say something on that swimming recording about a charity?'

'That's exactly what I was thinking.' I take out the pen and play it back to her. 'There's definitely something weird about this. We should look it up on the internet.'

'Okay, come back to my house after school,' says Sam. 'But we get the ruler and do the bag swap first.'

It feels pretty great to have a proper spy schedule. This must be what it's like when Mum and Dad talk to each other.

But the first stage of Operation Numbered doesn't go to plan. In fact, it doesn't go at all. At first break, Sam and I head over to the car park with the replacement bag tucked under Sam's arm, but as we come up to the gate, Sam swivels away from it and waves me back. 'He's in the car!'

We move as fast as we can so that we're not in view of the gate.

'I bet he's calling someone.' Then I remember what's in the car. 'That means another recording!'

'Operation Numbered will be re-launched at lunchtime,' Sam says.

I smile back at her. 'Right.'

We eat as fast as we can and are out in the

playground before anyone else. Unfortunately, so is Mr Caulfield.

'I'll keep him talking.' Sam thrusts the bag at me. 'You get the pen and do the switch.'

'What are you going to talk to him about?' I hiss.

'Our chances against St Colmer's.' Sam grins. 'And how brilliant my mum's article will be.'

I sprint over to the gate and then look over my shoulder. Sam's managed to get Mr Caulfield facing her, so his back is to me. She tugs her ear – our signal for *go ahead* – and I slip through into the car park before anyone notices me.

I unlock Mr Caulfield's car and put my hand down under the passenger seat to pick up the ruler. As I feel around for it, I touch a piece of paper that's dropped onto the floor. I glance at it and see the words *Start Sports* across the top. I stuff it into my bag and then find the ruler wedged under the mat. I'm about to pull out the *Bothen Hill News* bag that Sam's given me when I hear voices – Mrs Harrison and another teacher – discussing a staff meeting. I click the car door shut and crouch down, crawling round the side of the car so that I'm hidden from view and then lying flat on the tarmac. From underneath the car I see their feet disappearing through the gate. The gate swings shut after them but they don't move away! They stay there, chatting.

I can't risk doing the bag swap now. But I have to get back into school before anyone realises I'm gone. I crouch-run to the car park exit and lock the car before running along the pavement back to the front entrance to the school. A teaching assistant from the Reception class is on duty at the gate and when I tell her I've been collecting the packed lunch that I'd forgotten from my mum, she just waves me through.

'Where've you been?' Sam runs up to me. 'Did you manage it?'

'Only the ruler, not the bag. But don't worry, I've got an idea. I'll just have to bring in more gadgets.'

Sam raises her eyebrows. 'Good thing you're so well supplied.'

'I'd better put my bag back.' As a spy, you have to know how to deflect danger. In my case, that seems to mean changing the subject. A lot.

At football practice Mr Caulfield says I can be on the team for the match against St Colmer's. I'm not even a reserve!

Everything's brilliant until we have a break halfway through. I slump down next to Sam and don't notice my tracksuit bottoms have rucked up and my socks have rolled down. I only realise this when I see Sam staring – at my unusually hairy ankles. At my *incredibly-not-girly* hairy ankles.

'It's funny that you have dark hair on your legs when you're blonde,' she says, looking at me closely.

I thought she was going to say something about my legs being hairy – hairy enough to put-on-a-leash-and-take-for-a-walk hairy.

'Uh, yeah. It runs in the family. Different coloured hair.'

'I thought maybe you'd dyed it.'

'Course not!' My laugh doesn't sound that convincing. But that's because it's hard to sound like you think something's funny when you're terrified.

Sam puts her head to one side and studies my face.

'What is it?' I ask, not meeting her eyes.

'I don't know,' she says. 'Sometimes you remind me of something but I don't know what it is.' She stands up. 'Come on, Mr Caulfield's about to blow the whistle.'

I follow her onto the pitch, pushing down the panicky feeling in my stomach. I wonder if what Sam's being reminded of is *boy*, and what she senses is the something that tells you what you're looking at isn't really what it seems to be. If Sam is already starting to guess, how long do I have before everyone else does? Have my hairy ankles put our lives in danger?

Chapter 12

As soon as we're on the bus I pull out the piece of paper I found on the floor of Mr Caulfield's car. Underneath the *Start Sports* heading are various logos – a football being held up by kids, a tennis racket held by a large hand, a drawing of a girl in the starting position for a sprint. Then *Start Sports* typed in lots of different fonts. Underneath all that is an official-looking list of the Start Sports charity team. It's short. Very short. There's only one name: Mr N. Caulfield, Chief Executive.

'Mrs Harrison didn't say anything about Mr Caulfield being part of the charity.' Sam draws a circle in the fogged-up window.

'Maybe she doesn't know.'

We look at each other. Operation Numbered has moved up a gear.

I text Mum to let her know I'm going to Sam's. I'm a bit nervous about meeting Sam's mum in case she's like Melissa's mum and tries to give me some kind of makeover. But she hardly looks up from her computer. She just smiles, gives us a brief wave and tells us to help ourselves to biscuits. Her fingers are typing at about a million miles a minute.

'She wants to be promoted,' Sam tells me as we go upstairs. 'So she covers every story she can. But it's all stuff like the village fête or how local shops are being closed down. She needs a big story to get her noticed.'

'Maybe we'll be able to give it to her.'

Sam grins at me and pushes open the door to

her room. The walls are pale green and there's a dark green side table next to the bed. The curtains and duvet are both covered in some red and white spotty material and she has loads of posters of footballers.

'This is your room?' It can't be! It's normal!

'What's wrong with it?' Sam looks offended. 'You don't like it?'

'No, no, it's great. But it's – it's not pink.'

'Why would it be?'

'I just thought all girls . . .'

'What? That all girls like pink?' Sam raises her eyebrows. 'You really think that?'

'No. Of course I don't.' Yes, of course I do. 'Come on, let's listen to the new recording.' I make a big thing out of looking through my bag for the ruler even though I know exactly where I put it. By the time I pull it out, Sam seems to have forgotten about the pink comment. At least, I hope she has.

Even though it's voice-activated, the recorder isn't so clever that it picks up when people are having boring instead of important conversations.

We have to listen to ten minutes of Mr Caulfield organising a plumber for his leaking toilet and then calling a local gardening centre to find out what kind of vegetables are easiest to grow in a hot, dry climate.

'But where we live *isn't* hot and dry!' Sam points out.

Finally, we get to a conversation worth listening to.

'Recording started 10.31 a.m., Monday,' says the recorder.

'That's first break today!' I say. 'I knew he must be calling someone from the car.'

There's a bleep and then Mr Caulfield's voice. 'Mark, I've got the bank statements and the Start Sports papers. You're sure you can tidy them up?'

We can't really hear the other voice except as fuzzy static.

'Excellent. I've been doing very well with the grant-funding applications – everyone loves the idea of Start Sports,' Mr Caulfield's voice says. 'Encouraging health habits and community participation in sport – they're practically falling over themselves to give cash. And the football match will raise even more.'

More fuzzy static.

'I'll bring the papers in tomorrow and meet you after school. I want this sorted ASAP. Once the cash is all in the bank, why hang around?'

'Recording ended: 10.34 a.m., Monday,' the recorder says before clicking off.

'We have to get hold of those papers tomorrow,' says Sam. 'Before he gives them to whatshisface.'

'Definitely. But let's see what we can find out online.'

'Oh yeah.' Sam turns on a laptop and types *Start Sports* into Google.

There are a lot of links for starting stuff – diets, fitness routines, new jobs – and a lot of links for sports – rugby, football, basketball – but there's nothing about a charity called Start Sports.

'It doesn't exist,' Sam says. 'He's made up a charity to get people to give money to it. That means he's taking money away from Water Aid and Oxfam too because we usually raise money for them.'

'And it sounds like he's running off after the match.' I think for a second. 'I bet he's going somewhere that has a hot, dry climate.'

Sam scowls at the laptop as she shuts it down. 'We've got to stop him.'

Getting back into Mission Control that night isn't a problem. Dad's gone to do the shopping and Mum's having a bath after a long, hard day of surveillance. I pick up the disrupter and a couple of other things I think might come in handy the next day. In my old life, I used to know where Mum and Dad's chocolate stash was. In my new life, everything's been turned up a notch and I know where their spy gadget stash is. After working with Sam earlier, I almost feel like a real spy – and then I go into my room and see that my new dresses have arrived. *My new dresses.* They're not frilly and they're not pink but Dad's clearly making his girly girl point with the accessories. There are pink sparkly hair clips in the shape of a rabbit, a kitten, a puppy and a duck. They remind me that even though I have a spy mission, I am still dressing up as a girl. A girl with a small animal obsession.

I have to play an hour of Mega Tank on my phone before I feel even *close* to normal.

'You've got a pretty amazing collection of spy stuff,' Sam says the next morning on the bus after I've given her a glimpse inside my bag. 'You got it all from your parents?'

'No. Some of it I got with my pocket money. You know, online.'

That's the problem with lies. It's a bit like hiccoughs – once you start, it's hard to stop.

'You're funny,' Sam says. 'You *look* like the kind of girl Melissa is, but you don't *act* the same way girls like her usually do.'

'Haven't you ever heard of not judging a book by its cover?'

'You're not a book.'

'Yes, I am. I'm the girl version of Dan McGuire.'

She laughs, but all I can think is, *How long until she knows?*

I try not to worry about it. I need to focus.

Today, we're not taking any chances. We need two distractions, one so we can do the swap and the other so we can put the original bag back.

At first break, we take our positions. I sit on one of the benches by the main gate and select the fire alarm function on the disrupter in my rucksack and then tuck the rucksack under the bench. I get up and walk away from the bench with the remote control in my hand.

I look over at Sam and tug my ear. She nods.

I flick the switch on the remote and as the disrupter starts to shriek, Sam sprints off to the car park.

Everyone pours out of the building. Some people are shouting 'Fire!' and some are laughing, and a couple of Reception kids are in tears. Mrs Harrison is hurrying through the playground with her phone glued to her ear while the other teachers organise everyone in lines. As Mr Caulfield arrives to tick people off the register, I flick the alarm off and quickly retrieve my rucksack from under the bench. A second later, Sam's back, panting.

'Done?'

She turns to show the bag slung over her shoulder. 'Done.'

We stuff it into my rucksack and join the line for our class.

Mrs Harrison reappears, frowning. 'I don't understand, why has it just *stopped*? I was about to call the fire brigade.'

We have to stand around for ages while the teachers are talking about how the alarm didn't sound like the usual one and whether it's safe to go back inside. Then the caretaker appears and insists that the school fire alarm didn't go off at all. At last they decide that it must have been from the house next door to the school and after a while we all file back inside. Stage one of Operation Numbered is complete.

At lunch, while Sam keeps lookout, I lock myself in a toilet cubicle and photograph every document in Mr Caulfield's bag with one of Mum and Dad's miniature cameras. Mr Caulfield's bank statement shows loads and loads of entries under the deposit heading – all from Bothen Hill School. His total balance is over three hundred thousand pounds!

And there's another bank statement in the name of Start Sports – and the only contact listed is Mr Caulfield. I think we've got our proof now. As soon as I've finished, I stuff the papers back in the bag and come out.

'Right, let's get it back.'

I show Sam the disrupter and how to operate it. She whistles. 'I'm starting to think I shouldn't spend all my pocket money on chocolate.'

This time, we've decided on fireworks. Sam is setting the disrupter off in one of the toilets so that everyone assumes they can't see the fireworks because they're going off inside. I get out into the playground and as close as I can to the car park before she sets it off. At the first fizz and bang, I dash through the gate. Everyone turns and surges into school to find out what the noise is about. I unlock the car and do the bag swap in seconds. I'm almost out of the car park when I smack straight into Mr Caulfield.

My heart leapfrogs in my chest. 'Hello, sir.'

'Josie. What are you doing here?' Mr Caulfield is staring at his car.

'I heard all that noise in the school and it scared me. I guess I just ran.' I sound completely convincing. I used to be rubbish at lying but Josie is getting really good at it.

Except that Mr Caulfield doesn't look very convinced. He keeps glancing over at the car and then at me. 'What's that key for, Josie?'

 I'm still holding the multi-remote key! What was I thinking?

'It's my mum's. She lost it yesterday after she dropped me off.'

'I thought you said you ran here because you were scared? And how did your mum drive her car if she lost her key?'

Okay, maybe I need a bit of work on the lying front.

'She always keeps a spare in her bag because she loses it a lot. I ran here because I was scared and then saw the key.'

'I see.' Mr Caulfield keeps looking from me to the car. 'That's an interesting bag, Josie. I've got one just like it.'

I take a deep breath. I have to stay calm, just like Dan McGuire would. 'Yeah, Sam gave it to me. Her mum works for the *Bothen Hill News*.'

'So she does.'

There's this long, heart-beats-in-your-throat pause. After what feels like hours, Mr Caulfield says, 'Well, I think you'd better go back to the playground now. Whatever that noise was, it's over now.'

'Okay, sir. Thanks.' And then I *run*.

Not every spy mission can be expected to go perfectly.

Chapter 13

On the bus, I tell Sam what I saw in the bag.

'I can't believe he's really nicking all that money!' Sam's gone all red in the face. 'I *hate* liars. My dad was a liar. He lied about having an affair and Mum cried for about six months. We've got to show everyone what Mr Caulfield's really like. Who he really is.'

It makes me think of Sam finding out who I

really am. If she hates liars would she hate me?

I stop myself from thinking about it by telling her my idea of how to expose Mr Caulfield. Sam loves it. 'We're really going to stop him!'

It's only when I'm back at home that I start to worry. What if I didn't get the papers back in order and Mr Caulfield realises for sure that we're onto him? What if he tries to find out stuff about me – and he finds out about Mum and Dad and who we really are?

Though I can't help thinking that if we're captured, at least I wouldn't have to wear a skirt.

'You all right?' Dad peers at me across the table at dinner. 'Anything wrong at school? Did you see anything suspicious?'

I think about telling them everything but decide I won't unless I'm sure I've put us all in danger. If Sam and I can prove what Mr Caulfield is up to, Mum and Dad will have to realise I can spy like them. But maybe I should find out the consequences if we do get uncovered . . . just in case.

'If we get found out – about us not being who we're saying we are, I mean – could we be killed?'

'*Killed?*' Mum laughs. 'No, of course not! We would never be killed.' She puts her hand on top of mine and gives it a squeeze.

'Maybe sent to another country for a bit,' says Dad.

'Or detained in a security facility for a stretch,' adds Mum.

I want to be a professional football player in Brazil! That's not going to happen in a security facility!

'But no, we wouldn't be killed,' Dad says cheerfully.

My parents are such a comfort.

The next morning we're at school extra early to make sure we complete the next stage of our mission before registration. Luckily Mrs Harrison is already in and she loves our plan. She thinks we have 'initiative' and are full of 'community spirit'. All we have to do is go to the classroom and wait.

Mr Caulfield's finished taking registration when

Mrs Harrison taps lightly at the door.

'Mr Caulfield? May I come in a moment?'

'Of course, Mrs Harrison, come in, come in.'

'Josie and Sam were kind enough to let me tell you the wonderful news myself,' Mrs Harrison says.

'News? What news is that, Mrs Harrison?'

You can see from the way his eyes dart around the room that he's getting nervous.

'Your two students have come up with the brilliant idea of making a film about Start Sports! I'm making arrangements for it to be shown at the stadium before the game. Such initiative!'

Mr Caulfield doesn't say anything. He looks as if someone's rubbed ice all over his face.

'So of course they'll be wanting to talk to you, as you know so much about the charity. And perhaps you could even set up a few interviews with some of the people who actually run it?'

Mr Caulfield's still not speaking.

'Mr Caulfield?'

Mr Caulfield clears his throat. 'I think it might be difficult to set up the interviews with Start Sports in time – I mean, the match is in just a couple of days.'

'Oh surely they'll find someone to talk to us when we're doing so much to help highlight all they do and stand for? We'll be raising a lot of money for them after all!' Mrs Harrison sends Mr Caulfield another positive beam.

'They're a very small charity,' he says quickly. 'Just starting out. Small team, you know.'

'Oh. Well, I'm sure the girls can make do with an extra-long interview with you if that's the case.'

'The thing is, I don't know when I'll

be free, what with teaching, lesson-planning, marking, coaching the team for the match . . .'

'Oh, Mr Caulfield, *surely* you can spare just a few minutes for the girls? Josie and Sam have already gone to a lot of trouble to borrow filming and recording equipment. And after all, it is for *charity*.'

Mr Caulfield glances at the door as if he's considering making a run for it. 'Yes, all right then. Maybe we can do the interview at lunchtime. I'll be able to talk to the girls then.'

'Excellent! Come along to my office and I'll just squirrel myself away in a corner while you have the interview. I'm keen to hear all about this charity myself – as you've said, it's brand new!' Mrs Harrison laughs. 'Now I must let you get on with your lessons, everyone.'

She disappears and Mr Caulfield stares after her as if he's just been given some terrible news. Which he has really.

It's just as well I've done my last Mission Control raid for this operation. I heard Mum ask Dad this morning if he's been rearranging the gadget shelves. Still, it will all be worth it when we pull this off.

Mr Caulfield sits on a chair in Mrs Harrison's room for the interview, looking exactly like someone in one of the court dramas Dad used to watch – guilty.

Mrs Harrison watches on from the corner with a big smile on her face, already nodding in approval even though no one's said anything yet.

Sam positions the video camera and presses *Record*. 'So. When exactly did you find out about Start Sports, Mr Caulfield?'

'Um. I think I saw something about it in one of the football magazines.'

'And can you tell us a bit about how it works and why it's a good charity? Why we should be giving money to Start Sports instead of to Water Aid and Oxfam?'

'Yes, well . . .' Mr Caulfield coughs. 'It's about encouraging kids and adults to play sport and, you know, take part in the community.'

I take up the questioning. 'By playing sport?'

'Yeah. That's right.' Mr Caulfield nods several times like those bobbing-head toy dogs people put in the back of their cars.

'So they organise games, then?'

'Uh, yeah. That's right.' Mr Caulfield does some more nodding. Behind the camera, I see Sam trying to tuck away a smile.

'Where?'

'What?' Mr Caulfield shifts nervously in his seat.

'Where do they organise these games? I mean, because I'd really like to get involved.'

'The thing is,' Mr Caulfield says, glancing at the

camera, 'the charity's only just been put together. So, you know, some of this stuff hasn't happened yet.'

'Like the games.'

'Yeah.'

'So at the moment, they don't actually do anything.'

'Um, well.' Mr Caulfield coughs. 'As I said, things are at an early stage.'

I push on. 'You mean they haven't done any charity work yet.'

Mr Caulfield coughs again, his skin slowly turning a deep purple. 'Not as yet, not as such . . . no.' Confirmation – goal!

Mrs Harrison laughs. 'Now, Josie. Sorry, Sam, if you'd just like to put it on pause a moment.'

'Oh it doesn't matter, Miss, you can be in the film too.' Sam swings the camera over to her.

Mrs Harrison touches her hair. 'Oh. Well. As Mr Caulfield was saying, the charity has just been created. That's exciting in itself. After all, we as a school can be said to be helping it on its first steps – can't we, Mr Caulfield?'

'Yeah, that's right.' He's definitely sounding a bit queasy now.

'And who thought of it?' Sam smiles encouragingly. 'Who's the person behind it all?'

This is the question we've been working towards. I think of the charity account statement with only Mr Caulfield's name on it. If Mr Caulfield lies now, we've got him for sure. I hold my breath.

Mr Caulfield stares at Sam for a long second. 'Do you mean who runs it?'

'Yeah, runs it, had the idea, organises everything. You know.'

'Uh . . . right. Well. It's a woman called . . .' Mr Caulfield's eyes dart around the room. I see him stare at the clock over the door.

'Lesley Clock. Yeah, her name is Lesley Clock.'

Goal!

'Lesley *Clock*?' I have to bite the inside of my mouth to stop myself from laughing.

'Yeah, that's right.' A drop of sweat forms on his forehead and he reaches up to wipe it off.

'That's an unusual name,' Sam says, throwing me a quick smile. 'So who else runs it?'

Mr Caulfield forces out a laugh. 'Well, I can't know everything about the charity, you know, Sam – I don't run it myself!'

Hat-trick!

'I think that's enough for now in any case,' Mrs Harrison says. 'The bell's going to go in a moment and we must allow Mr Caulfield *some* time off for good behaviour!'

Sam and I exchange a look. If the rest of our mission goes to plan, Mrs Harrison is going to find out all about Mr Caulfield's behaviour . . .

Chapter 14

'Right, go and get changed for PE, everyone.' Mr Caulfield sounds a bit snappy but that's to be expected. Criminals do get jittery when they're under attack. It's how Dan McGuire always knows he's on the right track.

I'm heading down the corridor when Mr Caulfield calls after me. 'Where are you going, Josie?'

'Just to the toilet, sir.'

'There's a toilet next to the changing room.'

Up to now, I've got away with changing in the toilets furthest away from the changing room, and apart from the one walk-through at the leisure centre, I've managed to avoid the whole getting-undressed-in-front-of-other-people question altogether. I'm about to play my shy card when I see the look in Mr Caulfield's eye. He's not in the mood to be understanding.

'Come on, Josie. Get moving.'

It's too bad we're not doing athletics today. I am so ready to run.

I'm in for a shock when I get to the changing room. The toilet next to it has a large sign hanging on the door – *Out of Order*. I feel a bubble of panic rise up in me. I turn to try and go back to the other toilets but now I'm surrounded by girls, all talking and laughing as they push through the changing room door.

'Come on, Josie, get a move on!' Melissa pulls at my sleeve.

I've got no choice but to follow her. As soon as

I'm inside, I realise this isn't PE, it's biology.

'Are you all right?' Sam slings her bag on the hook over the bench.

'Fine.' I look round desperately. Where's the cubicle for shy girls to change in? There's nowhere to hide. It's like one of those nature programmes when they film the prey of a predator in the wild. And guess who's the deer staring into the lion's massive mouth?

Sam starts pulling off her jumper. No! Not Sam!

My skin feels like it's been lit with a match. I keep my eyes down and try to ignore what's happening around me. Everyone is tugging off skirts and tops and tights. Everyone's flinging clothes around and chatting as if it's all perfectly normal. Nerida's not just talking about her bra, she's getting everyone to *look at it* and tell her how pretty it is. What's *wrong* with her? Boys don't go round getting people to admire their underpants! I keep my eyes locked on my bag and take out my tracksuit bottoms. At least I won't have to change my top as I have a long-sleeved T-shirt under my school jumper. Why didn't Mum and Dad plan for this?! What kind of spies do they think they are? They can't even protect their son from having to get changed in front of millions of girls!

I can't think of one single situation that Dan McGuire's ever faced that's worse than this. That bit in *Dan McGuire and the Fiery Flames* when he has to walk through a burning building that's been doused in petrol? Or *Dan McGuire and the Rasp of the Rattle* when he's dropped into a cauldron of snakes? Or when he has to dive under an ice floe and swim away from a pod of killer whales? Nothing. *Nothing* compared to this.

'Josie? Are you okay?' Melissa peers into my face. Great, now everyone's looking at me.

'I'm fine. Just – I'm just —' *About to throw up.*

Melissa goes away and I

wriggle out of my tights without taking off my skirt. Then I lean over and yank up my tracksuit bottoms before anyone can get a load of my hairy legs.

'Whoa! Josie!'

Oh no. Here we go. Deportation city. The cover's blown. Someone's seen the giveaway legs and put them together and added up to JOSIE'S A BOY. What's going to happen to me and Mum and Dad? I've ruined everything!

Someone's hand tugs at my exposed waistband. 'Boxer shorts?!'

I twist round to see Nerida's mouth stretched out in a delighted grin. '*Boxer* shorts?! I've seen boxer-style *knickers* but these are *proper* boxers. You must be totally boy mad!'

I tug down my T-shirt. I'd like to say something clever, but my brain's on strike.

'Don't you know anything, Nerida?' Sam appears in front of me. 'Boxers are the new thing. My mum's doing a piece about film stars wearing their boyfriend's boxers in the paper. It's *huge* in Hollywood,' she says.

I stay very still.

Nerida's grin freezes. 'Oh.'

'Yeah. Surprised none of you knew about it.'

'Why aren't *you* wearing them then?' asks Nerida.

Shut up, bra-face.

'Just waiting for them to arrive,' Sam says casually. 'My mum ordered me some online on Saturday.'

'Oh.'

It's the 'oh' of defeat. It's the sound of that 'oh' that makes me realise my boy butt is saved.

'That's so cool!' Melissa says. 'I'll get some at the weekend!'

'Me too!'

And suddenly there's a chorus of voices, all talking about how they're going to get themselves some boxer shorts as soon as they can.

Sam's saved me from discovery and created a

new fashion craze all at the same time.

But do I thank her? Do I even look at her as we make our way out of the changing room and into the playground? No, I do not. Not because I'm not grateful. I am. I realise how good a friend Sam is more every day. How much I'll miss her if I get taken away with Mum and Dad. No, it's not because I don't want to thank her that I'm not looking at her. It's because I'm wondering why she covered up for me as if she knew what I've got to hide.

Sam doesn't talk to me during PE. She doesn't talk to me in the changing room. She doesn't talk to me while we work on our history project, Exploring the Vikings, or when the bell goes for end of school. She doesn't talk to me on the bus, or when we get off.

But just outside my house she whips round to face me.

'You're a boy, aren't you?'

I give it one last go. 'What?!'

'You're a boy disguised as a girl.'

'You're mad.'

'Hairy ankles, boxer shorts, big feet. Allergic to water and make-up. Loves football and Mega Tank but wears sparkly *bunny rabbit* clips in her hair and thinks girls only like pink. *How likely is that?*'

'Everyone's different!'

Sam looks at me. 'Shall I give that hair a tug?'

'No!' I slam a hand to the top of my head to protect myself. It's bad enough that Sam's guessed, but if she says anything, or if anyone else does . . .

'I thought maybe it was true but I wasn't sure. Even though there were so many signs, I trusted you. That was stupid, wasn't it?' She looks away, chewing on her bottom lip.

I step towards her even though she immediately backs away. 'No, you see, there's a reason – but I can't tell you what it is. But it's really important, Sam, you have to believe me.'

'I don't care what the reason is. I. Don't. Like.

Liars.' Sam takes another step back.

'Sam, wait!'

She puts her hands on her hips. 'What did you do it for? A bet? A dare? A laugh?'

'You've got to be kidding me. You think I'd do it for a laugh? Why would I *want* to be a girl?'

Sam narrows her eyes. 'What's so bad about being a girl?'

'Nothing. Nothing!'

Sam stares at me as if she doesn't know me.

'Let me explain.' I don't know what I'm going to say. I can't tell her the truth, but I hate seeing the expression in Sam's eyes. Like she can't stand to look at me.

'I don't want to talk to you right now.' Sam's eyes well up. 'What kind of friend lies to you like that? What kind of friend do you think you are?' She spins round on her heel and runs off.

Every day I've been thinking that having to dress up as a girl is the worst thing that's ever happened to me. As I watch Sam slam the door of her house behind her, suddenly I'm not so sure.

Chapter 15

I work until really late on the Start Sports documentary. I can at least make sure that the rest of Operation Numbered goes to plan, even if my real mission has failed. I try to convince myself Sam won't give me away. If she covered up for me in PE, doesn't that mean she understands that it's important – even if she doesn't know why? But if she *does* tell . . . we'll be in real danger. My stomach churns as I put the film together.

When Eddie and I used to have fights, we'd shout and maybe push each other about. Sometimes we might not speak to each other for an hour, but it didn't usually last because we'd get bored or forget why we were annoyed. Mind you, we would be arguing about which one of us was better at football, or whether Quavers are better than Pringles, or which was the best ever episode of *Doctor Who*. We never had an argument about one of us pretending to be something they weren't. Like a girl. So maybe it's normal that I'm a lot more bothered than I ever was when Eddie and I had a fight.

Sam likes the same stuff I do and doesn't make fun of me all the time like Eddie did. She doesn't boast about the stuff she's good at the way he did. And she's stuck by me and got me out of trouble even though she didn't have to.

She's been a better friend to me than Eddie ever was, and now I've messed it up.

Of course Sam isn't at the bus stop the next morning. She must have left early or got her mum to give her a lift. I don't see her until I get into class, and when I sit down she doesn't look at me once.

I finally corner her in the corridor at break. 'Can I talk to you for a second?'

'Do you want to go in here, or there?' Sam jerks her head towards the boys' toilets.

'Shhh, please.' I glance around to see if anyone's heard her. This could be disastrous. I could be on my way to some high-security facility with Mum and Dad by this afternoon – or worse – if Sam decides to tell everyone. I tug at her sleeve and lead her into the girls' toilets. Luckily, they're empty.

Sam leans against the sink and folds her arms across her chest. 'What do you want?'

'I'm really sorry I lied to you. You've got to believe me, I'm not doing this because I want to. It's because I have to.'

'You *have* to lie?'

'It's not just me. It's my mum and dad too.'

'What – your mum's a man and your dad's a woman?'

'No! I mean we'd all be in danger if it got out that I'm not a girl.'

Sam just raises an eyebrow.

This isn't going well. I appeal to her sense of justice.

'What about Operation Numbered? We need to make sure everyone knows what Mr Caulfield's done.'

'Oh. Right. We have to uncover Mr Caulfield's lies. But it's okay for *you* to lie.'

'But I'm not stealing anything from anyone! I'm not hurting anyone by dressing like a girl!'

'No? What about *me*?'

The bell rings and Sam swings out of the toilets without another word.

I end up with Melissa and Nerida and Suzy in the playground at lunchtime. I watch Sam having a kick about and wish I could join in.

'Did you have a fight with Sam?' Nerida hops up on the wall and swings her legs.

'Well, obviously she did,' Melissa says. She gives me a sympathetic look. 'What was it about, Josie? Maybe we can help.'

'Nothing. I mean, I don't know.'

'Do you want to come over after school? We could do each other's nails and watch *Dance to the Stars*.'

'Thanks, but I can't.' I don't mention I'd rather be left in London Zoo's lion enclosure covered in raw steak.

Mr Caulfield is off during the afternoon. Mrs Harrison says he's got a lot to organise before the match tomorrow. I can't help glancing over at Sam when she says that. I bet he's booking his flights to Mexico or the Canaries or wherever he's decided to run away to with his stolen money. But Sam keeps looking straight ahead.

It's weird, because ever since I've had to dress like a girl, I haven't wanted anyone to look at me, and now Sam won't and I'd do anything to make her turn round.

I can't even think of a situation that Dan McGuire has been in that's like this. Probably because Dan McGuire doesn't have any friends.

He should. Everyone needs one.

I've basically given up when Sam comes up to me after school at the bus stop.

'I'm not going to tell anyone about you.' She holds up her hand before I can say anything. 'But I won't help you with Operation Numbered unless you do the right thing at the match.'

'What do you mean?'

'That's what you've got to figure out.'

'What —'

'That's all you get. See you later.' Sam stalks past me, leaving me staring after her.

I have absolutely no idea what she wants me to do.

Chapter 16

I don't think I've ever slept so badly – not even the first night after I found out I had to become 'Josephine'. I keep thinking about the plan and what will happen if it goes wrong – which it will if I can't figure out what Sam wants me to do. But it's not just the operation going wrong that I'm worried about. If I don't get Sam to forgive me, she won't be my friend again, and if she won't be my friend again then I really can't stand this Josie cover any more. It's like that thing about how every dog year is seven human years. Every Josie day is like a year of my old life.

And then, just as it's getting light, I get it. It's not so much like a light bulb flashing as being washed all over in sunlight. I can't believe it took me so long to figure it out! It's a good punishment too. But it's worth it if it means Sam will be on my side again.

Now I can enjoy every minute of the day, every minute of exposing Mr Caulfield for the fraud he is – while my fraud stays securely hidden under my skirt.

I spring out of bed to check the weather – the one thing we can't control is a cancellation because of rain. But the sunshine's flooding into my room. For the first time I don't even mind fixing my wig and putting on my skirt and tights. Josie's not so bad. After all, without her, none of this would be about to happen.

* * *

The match has been scheduled for late morning, so when I get to school the team is already boarding the coach that Mrs Harrison's organised. Everyone's chattering like mad. I don't manage to get a seat next to Sam so I can't tell her I know what to do. I do flash her a grin though. She looks away, but I can tell she wants to smile back. That's the thing about friends – you have a secret code. Just like spies do.

The stadium is amazing. The pitch – a professional pitch! – is so green it's practically shining. I can't help imagining what it would be like to score a goal in a stadium like this.

As everyone exclaims over the pitch and asks where the changing rooms are and if they can eat their lunch early, I go up to Sam. 'I think I know what I have to do.'

Sam slings her bag over her shoulder and waits.

 I lower my voice so no one else can hear. I take a breath.

This isn't as easy to say as I thought it would be. I've been dreaming of playing in a proper stadium all my life. It would have been blinding to be on that pitch. I'm about to volunteer to kick my dream into touch.

But Sam's right. 'I'm not playing in the match,' I tell her, 'because I'd be stopping one of the real girls from getting a chance to play.'

A smile spreads across Sam's face. 'Congratulations.' She hoists her bag further up her shoulder. 'Now come on, we've got an operation to get underway.'

I put the small black box in place during a carefully timed toilet break while Sam keeps a lookout. I'm hoping the new gadgets from Mission Control are as good as they look. If I've read the instructions properly, the little black box

I found is going to be even more effective than the disrupter.

Then we deliver the film to Mrs Harrison, and all that's left to do is wait. And tell Mr Caulfield that he needs a new player. I wait until the St Colmer's team have arrived and the warm-ups begin. A few people are filing through to take their seats.

'Mr Caulfield?'

'Yes, Josie?'

'I'm sorry, sir, but I can't play today.'

'What?'

'I was just warming up and I turned my ankle, sir. It really, really hurts.' I pinch the inner skin of my wrist to make my eyes well up and make my mouth tremble as if I'm about to cry.

Then Sam comes running up as arranged. 'Evie

 can play, Mr Caulfield. She's a really good reserve and she's already wearing her kit.'

'I know who the reserves are, Sam,' Mr Caulfield says.

You can see him wondering if this is something to worry about. He shrugs. I think he's decided he's got enough to worry about already.

'Go and rest your ankle then, Josie.'

I get myself out of the way, whispering 'Good luck' to Sam.

She mouths, 'You too,' and gives me a thumbs up.

I make my way into the stands and find a seat at the end of an aisle. Mr Caulfield blows a whistle and the two teams run out onto the pitch.

From the start, it's clear that the visiting team have no chance. Evie is dominant on the ball and crosses it to Sam four times in the first ten minutes. Sam scores – once on the first try, sneaking it into the left corner of the goal, and then again at the third chance by booting it straight past the opposition goalie. The school goes wild after the second goal.

You have to give St Colmer's credit for trying. They manage to get possession of the ball and kick it upfield. But then Sam darts up the pitch, cuts in and takes it back to where it belongs – in goal. The score is three–nil to us! I'm not even sure Dan McGuire could score this many goals. Well, okay, maybe he could, but he's got the advantage of not being real.

A man next to me shakes his head. 'They're very good for a girls' team.'

I glare at him. 'They're just brilliant. Full stop.'

'No, no, of course, yes, that's right, they are.' The man coughs.

Finally, the whistle blows for half-time. It's time for the last stage of Operation Numbered to get underway.

Mrs Harrison appears carrying a microphone and nearly trips as she sets it up. Really, I should have lent her the stylus issue mic that Dad showed me. Full stadium coverage in a brooch or tie clip you can fasten to your shirt or jacket.

Mrs Harrison taps the microphone and clears her throat. 'Ladies and gentlemen, girls and boys. We are delighted to be here in order to raise funds for a very special cause, one that is close to the hearts of all those at Bothen Hill School.'

Close to our hearts? Close to Mr Caulfield's wallet more like.

'The job of telling you about Start Sports, the charity we are all here to support, has been taken on by two enterprising and creative young girls at our school, Sam and Josie. They kindly volunteered to make a special film about Start Sports so that you can all see where your donations have gone.'

The crowd of parents and friends of the schools gives her a round of applause.

Mrs Harrison smiles and gestures to the screen. 'So without further ado, let's find out all about Start Sports!'

I crane my neck to see Mr Caulfield. He's taken a seat a few rows up from me. He's looking pretty relaxed, probably because he figures he'll be safely far away soon. Not soon enough, though.

Maybe I shouldn't say so myself but the film is completely professional. When we get to the bit where Mr Caulfield says the Chief Executive of the charity is Lesley Clock it cuts away to a shot of the Start Sports' official list of employees. Then it slowly zooms in on the only name on the list: Mr Caulfield.

There's a gasp from everyone in the stands but the film's already moved on to the bank statements – zooming in on the name at the top again and again: Mr Caulfield, Mr Caulfield, Mr Caulfield.

Operation Numbered is accomplished. As a bonus, I finally know how Dan McGuire feels when he's finished a mission. Blinding. Absolutely blinding.

It's not quite over, though, because Mr Caulfield decides to make a run for it. Not that he can run very far. Or very fast. For a football coach, he's really unfit.

It doesn't matter how fast he is anyway because

we're ready for him. As he crosses the pitch, I take out the remote for the small black box I've installed near the exit. As Mr Caulfield tries to go through I flip the first switch. A trip wire springs up, making Mr Caulfield stumble. I flip the second switch. The box releases a wide net that drops over Mr Caulfield and then clicks into place at his ankles.

'That's very clever, that.' Sam appears at my side. 'What about the police?'

I point over at Mrs Harrison. She is jabbering into her mobile and waving her free arm about.

'Won't they wonder where that net came from?' Sam asks.

'Oh don't worry about that. It's designed to dissolve after about twenty minutes. By the time the police get here there will be nothing left.'

'Where *did* that net come from?'

'My dad works in security.' It's *kind* of true.

'Right.' Sam punches me in the upper arm. 'Anyway, well done, Josie. That wasn't bad at all . . .' She lowers her voice to a whisper. '. . . for a *boy*.'

Chapter 17

Watching Mr Caulfield being taken away by the police is completely brilliant. He keeps trying to blame other people. At one point he even says it was all Mrs Harrison's idea. Which is pretty stupid considering Mrs Harrison was in charge of screening our documentary.

As arranged, Sam does all the talking to the police about the film. She's even agreed to say we 'found' the papers. Since her mum is being promised a raise and promotion to chief reporter because of the story, she's really happy.

The only tricky bit is when I have to go home and tell Mum and Dad about what's happened. Even though I've finally got proof that I can be a good spy, I can't be sure how they'll take it. So I talk fast and try to skim over the times where I nearly got caught. The only bit I leave out is Sam knowing the truth about my cover. She's promised she won't tell anyone and I trust her. And there's no point adding to Mum and Dad's stress levels.

After I've finished, there's this long pause. They're both looking their most spy-like. Dad stares at all the equipment I borrowed that I've put on the table. Mum stares at Dad.

'How did he get hold of all of this, Jed?'

'You knew I was showing him round.'

'You weren't supposed to show him the entry code!'

'I didn't!'

Some parents argue about the washing up. My

parents argue about who's let the Mission Control pass code slip.

'It's not Dad's fault. I spied on him,' I tell them.

They both swivel round to look at me.

'What? It's just what you do all the time!'

Dad laughs. 'Genes will out, Zelia.'

Mum shakes her head but she's smiling. 'I suppose it ended well.'

'We're proud of you.' Dad says. 'But next time, *ask* before you borrow.' He picks up the recording Tipp-Ex and taps the lid. 'It's expensive stuff.'

'There's not going to be a next time,' Mum says. 'From now on we're playing by the book and *keeping in the background*.'

Keeping in the background works up until Sam calls round. I've told Mum and Dad that I have to be able to have a friend round now and then to cope with my cover. Dad answers the door.

'Hello, Mr Marcus, Mrs Marcus.'

'Please. Call me . . .' Dad stops. His face looks blank, and then takes on a look of panic. I guess he's still a bit thrown by everything I've told him.

'Oh it's all right, I know they're not your real names anyway,' Sam says.

There's a silence. Sam smiles cheerfully at them.

'Excuse me?' Dad looks from Sam to me, and back again.

I shake my head to show it's nothing to do with me.

'Don't worry,' Sam says. 'I won't tell anyone.'

'Tell them what, Sam?' Mum sits down on the sofa.

'That the three of you are spies.'

Sam thinks I'm a real spy!

'What?!' Mum sits bolt upright, her eyes fixed on Sam's face.

'I only guessed because I've got to know Josie so well. Nobody else would know. And anyway – a recording football, pen and ruler? A device that sets off burglar alarms and fireworks? A remote-controlled trip wire and net?'

'I do work in security, Sam,' Dad says.

'With a net that *dissolves*?'

'Jed . . .' Mum's voice is very low, with a hum of menace in it. 'You said that we'd be *one hundred per cent* safe.'

'We are!' he says. Then he looks down. 'We were.'

'Honestly, don't worry. I won't tell anyone,' Sam says again.

'I really can't tell you how important it is that you don't.' Mum gives Sam her best Serious Spy look. She's obviously given up on denying it.

'Sure.'

'So what do we do now?' Mum runs her hand through her hair, looking worried. 'Maybe we should ask HQ to leave earlier than planned. It's not fair to ask Sam to carry such a big secret.'

'Oh it's no problem. I'm good at it, aren't I, Josie?'

I grin at her. They have no idea how good.

'And anyway,' Dad says, 'we haven't finished *our* operation yet, Zelia.'

'We could help,' Sam says.

We all look at her.

'I mean, we did really well with Mr Caulfield, didn't we? Why can't Josie and I do more jobs like that?'

'That's a *blinding* idea!' I say.

'All right, Josie.' Mum shoots me a *that's enough* look.

'Come on, Mum. You've got to admit, no one will ever suspect two *kids*.'

Mum and Dad look at each other, first in shock. Then the shock melts into something else – a sense of thinking it over, of possibility.

Dan McGuire, secret agent, spy genius, is fiction. But maybe Josie, undercover boy, secret spy, is about to become fact.

It might just make it worth being her for a bit longer.

Won't it?

Coming Soon

Spies in Disguise

Boy
in a Tutu

To keep his family safe, Joe must still convince
the world he is 'Josie'. At least his life is
more fun now Sam knows his secret,
and when they discover a plot, they must put
their spy skills to the test.
The new mission? To go undercover
in the dance school show and find out what the
mysterious Mrs Rushka is up to.
But Joe's mortified to discover that he'll be
playing the female lead! Can he keep it together
long enough to unmask the villain?

piccadillypress.co.uk/children

Go online to discover:

☆ more books you'll love

☆ competitions

☆ sneak peeks inside books

☆ fun activities and downloads